MW01702205

BRUISED BUT NOT Broken

JOHN D. MCCRAY

ASPIRE
PUBLISHING HUB LLC.

Bruised but not Broken

ISBN
978-1-962611-61-9 (Paperback)
978-1-962611-62-6 (eBook)
978-1-962611-60-2 (Hardcover)

Dedication

First and foremost, I would like to thank God for blessing me with my special talent to be able to write my sixth book. I would like to thank my mom and dad for always encouraging me to do my best in whatever I do in life. I would like to thank my siblings for always supporting me, Lamont, Brian, Shakelia, Tyra and Leana. I would also like to thank some special people that always gave me that extra push that I needed when I felt like giving up and has supported me from day one; Erica Capers, Matthew Collins, Misa Griffin, Anitra Hammett, Sylinda F. Johnson, Angela Richburg, and Lawanda Samuels. I would like to thank two great people who are no longer here and are looking down on me from above. Thank you both for your support through the years and you are definitely missed Lee Pickens, and Tyrone Fogle. Last but not least, I would like to thank my grandparents who are no longer here, the late John and Daisy Carraway and Richard and Ida Mae McCray. Thank you all for your love through the years. You are definitely appreciated.

Table of Contents

CHAPTER

1

A BEAT DOWN

I sat on the edge of the bed watching TV, when I heard Jason's phone ringing on top of the dresser. Jason was in the shower. I walked towards his phone and looked at the screen, Marcus was calling. I held his phone in my hand debating on whether I should answer it because something told me that this wasn't Marcus calling.

I answered the phone but decided to deepened my voice, pretend to be him. "Hello," I answered. "Hey sweetie. Are you on your way?" the woman asked. "Yeah. I'll be there in about thirty minutes," I said, still trying to disguise my voice. "Good baby. I'll see you shortly," the woman said before she hung up.

I pressed end on his phone and placed it back on the dresser like Jason had it. The shower water stopped and I sprinted back over to the bed. I still had on my jeans and tee-shirt from earlier today, I was thinking about jumping in the shower but that quickly changed when I answered Jason's phone.

Jason walked out the bathroom completely naked. I turned around to look at him and it took everything in me to not walk up to him and slap the shit out of him. This fool was cheating on me again. After being married for ten years and having two children and he's doing this shit again.

Jason is the pastor of Red Hill Baptist church, one of the largest African American churches in the Gastonia area. We have over three to four thousand members that attend every Sunday for service. How can this man pretend to be a man of God, preaching and shouting every Sunday on the pulpit, knowing he's doing what he's doing? Jason has to be one of the phoniest pastors I've ever seen. Jason can barely hold his bible in his hand or keep his dick in his pants for that matter to even preach the word of God.

Jason pulled out some underwear from the top drawer along with some socks. "Where are you going?" I asked, looking him up and down. I'm going to a card game at Marcus house," Jason said, throwing on some jeans and a tee-shirt. "Okay, can I come?" I asked. "No. It's just us men hanging out. We just going to play some poker and maybe a few games or spades. We might have a few beers as well. You know just hanging out with the guys," Jason said. "Okay. Cool," I replied.

I watched Jason finished getting dress and splashing cologne on his face. Why the hell does he need to put cologne on to hang out with the fellas for? Jason grabbed his Atlanta Braves hat and put it on and then grabbed his car keys. "Baby, I'll see you shortly. I won't be out too long," Jason said, kissing me before heading out the door.

As soon as Jason walked out the door, I grabbed my sneakers and quickly put them on. I grabbed my car keys as well and headed out the door. I waited for him to pull all the way out the driveway before I got in my car to follow him. Jay and Myra are in their bedrooms watching TV. I didn't have time to tell them I'm stepping out for a few minutes and I'll be back later. I just won't stay out too long and they won't know that I left them alone.

Here I am, driving through my home town of Gastonia, North Carolina, to catch my cheating husband in another one of his sinful affairs. I made sure to stay my distance from following too close behind Jason. After all, the last thing I needed him to notice that I'm following him, even though I doubt if he would notice me, since he's too busy trying to meet up with his little side chick. This isn't Jason's first or second affair that I caught him in but I promise you this will be his last one that I'm going to deal with.

Jason pulled up to a small brick house and got out the car, carrying a black duffle bag. His car was parked beside a dark blue Chevy Malibu. I guess that's the little skank's car he's messing with.

I took out my phone and took a picture of Jason and the woman's car in front of the house. I made sure to get a picture of the lady's license plate as well. I'll have Lamar check this out for me tomorrow in case I want more details about the woman. Lamar is a trustee at our church and he has a little soft spot for me. Lamar told me a long time ago if I ever get tired of Jason cheating on me and want a good loyal man, call him.

I'm sure a lot of people at our church knows Jason is cheating, but no one said anything to me. My two best friends Sharese and Adrienne, always keeps me in the loop, whenever they hear and find out things, but most the time Jason ass is the one that gives it away every time. I heard something on one of Tyler Perry's play, as he played Madea. Madea said "A man can't cheat better than a woman can. Some kind of way, a man is going to do something to give themselves up," and I'll be damn if that's not the truth.

I think the first time, I found a ladies one earring in Jason's car and a tube of lipstick. Jason swear it was mine but I knew it wasn't, because I don't wear lipstick, I wear gloss. I let Jason think he won that argument but of course I didn't let it go. Then I started finding credit card receipts in his pocket for the "Red Roof Inn" and "Best Western Hotel." I kept all those receipts in a little envelope in my keepsake box, that I have in the top of my closet. I also would hear his late midnight phone calls and text messages he's been getting that he tried keeping it on vibrate or silent, so I wouldn't hear it, which I always did.

I looked down at my watch and it was nine-forty-five. I know damn well I'm not going to be out here all night. I'm going to walk around the house to see if I can see something. I hope she or her neighbors doesn't have any vicious dogs or anything. The last thing I'm about to be doing is running from some German Shepherd or a Pit Bull jumping over fences, praying and screaming that the dog doesn't bite me.

This is ridiculous, I just followed my husband to this tramp's house, waiting for him to come out. Why do I need to clarify what I already know what's going on? I guess I need this one last time to see for myself. This is the last straw for mc.

I grabbed my phone off the passenger side and was about to get out the car, until this white car flew pass me into the driveway behind the lady's car. The person turned off the headlights before they parked. I know that sign all too well. My ass was looking so hard out my window that if someone came up behind me and yelled "boo," I would probably piss myself. I wind my window all the way down, holding my phone in my hand. "Jason is about to get his ass beat. Jason is about to get his ass beat." I started singing over and over again, like I was singing a children nursery or something.

The man got out the white Cadillac Deville and gently shut his car door. Hot damn this shit is about to be so damn good. This man had to be about 6'2, and two hundred and fifty pounds of muscle. Jason is only about 5'10 and one hundred and sixty pounds, soak and wet. The man looked solid, like he could body slam Jason with his eyes closed.

I knew what time it is when he gently closed his car door. This man didn't want to give himself away at all. He wanted to pop up on them like a tornado, with no warning and I couldn't wait to get my front row seat. Hell it's been months since I've seen a good movie but something tells me a sister was going to see a live WWF Smack down match.

I got out my car and ran up to the front door. The door wasn't even closed all the way. I guess the man still didn't want them knowing he was there until he was ready to. I peaked in the door and the man looked like he ran from the kitchen and was heading down the hallway. Now I know I had to be good and crazy for walking in these people house, who I don't know like I live here or something. I actually wanted to go down the hallway to the bedroom but I think I'll just stay my ass right here, just in case I have to run if bullets start flying. I know they say that curiosity killed the cat but from the size of that man, he was going to dammit destroy whatever he found.

All I heard was "boom, boom, boom!" and a woman screaming "Stop Allan! Stop Allan! You're going to kill him!" Lord it took everything in me to not run down that hallway to see this man having my husband balled up, ready to throw him out the window. "Bitch! You screwing this man up in my house and in my damn bed! I should beat your ass too! You better be glad I'm a damn man and you're a woman, otherwise I would give you what I'm giving your little damn punk ass boyfriend right now. A damn beat down!" I wanted to run down the hallway again just to tell the man, "no, I'll beat her ass, you just beat on my husband," but I wasn't that stupid. Shit, I've only been in one fight my whole life and that was when my chubby cousin Keisha, stole my Oreo cookies from me and ate them in my face. "Lord I sure wish I could be damn Laila Ali right now, and box that ass up right quick."

I heard the door open to the bedroom and I hauled ass back outside and jumped off the front porch. The man burst out the screen door and through Jason off the porch, like a little rag doll. Jason did have on his briefs and a tee-shirt so it was good he wasn't out here butt ass naked fighting.

The man and the lady saw me standing in the yard looking. "Lady, who the hell are you? You one of our nosey ass neighbors that came to see what all the commotion is about before you call the police, screaming?" The man yelled. "No! I'm this man's wife that saw you through my husband off the porch." I said. "Hell, he better be glad that's all I did. He's up in my house, fucking my wife and in my bed. He better be glad his ass is still alive." The man said.

I heard everything the man said and the woman was standing in the yard looking scared, as if she was afraid her husband was going to turn on her next. "Now what are you going to do with your wife since you can't hit her? She was the one who invited him in your house. He didn't break in there." I said. "Why you want some of her for sleeping with your husband? Trust me sweetheart, she's all yours." The man said, pushing her in front of him.

I took off my hoodie and ran towards her with all my damn might, knocking her to the ground. Hell, I felt like a defensive line backer the way I tackled her ass to the ground. I started punching, wailing, stumping, and kicking her slutty ass like she was a piece of trash on the street. I took all my frustration out on her for what my husband was doing with her. It was only fair if my husband was getting his ass beat, which he deserved, then she was going to get her ass beat as well. "Damn shorty, I see you. Beat her ass! She was fucking your husband in our house, beat her trifling ass. Especially since I can't do it." The man yelled.

I finally stopped wailing on the woman but not until I saw blood. I was all wet up in my sweat, spit, and even my damn tears. Why was I fighting this woman like she was the one who took vowels with me ten years ago, before our family, friends and God. She wasn't the one I had two children with and build a home with. She wasn't the one I was sleeping with every night and she wasn't the one who cheated on me. But I still was going to beat her whorish ass though. After I was done with her I walked over to Jason while he was still lying on the ground holding his stomach and I hauled off and kicked the shit out of him and now I was done. "Damn girl, You a bad ass chick. I mean you was about your business I see," the man said.

I smiled at the man's comment as I walked back towards my car and drove off, without saying a word to anyone. If I wasn't sure about anything before, I knew my marriage was over for good.

CHAPTER

2

I KNOW MY WORTH

I just pulled up in my driveway, staring as if I was looking out of space, wondering where things went wrong in our marriage. I always knew that Jason had a wandering eye but Lord, I had no idea he had a wandering dick as well, until five years ago.

I remember when I was at work in the breakroom eating my lunch, when someone called me on my lunchbreak and told me if I wanted to know where my husband is, go to Super 8 on Hampton avenue at room sixty-seven. I told Adrienne one of my best friends, who is also the principal at the elementary school that I worked at that I had and emergency and had to leave for a little while. Adrienne told me that was fine for me to leave.

Until this day, I never knew who called me or how they got my number, but I was grateful. Just as I got to the hotel, the young lady and Jason was walking out the room. I got out the car so fast, I thought I pulled a muscle. Jason and the woman stopped dead in their track when they saw me. I walked up to them and slapped the shit out of her first and then slapped the shit out of him and left. I told Adrienne and Sharese what happened, and they both teased me and said I didn't handle it like a real sister. I asked what they meant by that? Sharese said a real sister would've grabbed that heifer by her hair and dragged her all over the damn parking lot, letting everyone see the homewrecker she really is and when I got tired of dragging her, beat the shit out of her. I told them both that I wasn't going to jail behind causing a scene in a hotel parking lot and lose my job behind it. The devil is a liar. How would that look on the front page paper, "Third grade teacher and First Lady of Red Hill Baptist Church, fighting cheating husband's mistress on hotel parking lot?" I wasn't going to do all that.

I eventually let Jason come back home after three months of being separated. Jason promised me he was going to do better and he hasn't. His affairs kept going on and now I'm done with him and his whores.

I walked inside and Jay was sitting at the table drinking some water. "Hey Mom. I didn't know you were gone. Where is Dad?" Jay asked. "I don't know son but I guess he'll be back in a little while. Look, I'm a little tired so I'm turning in for the night." I said, grabbing about six garbage bags from the cabinet. "Okay Mom. Have a goodnight." Jay said. "You too sweetheart and after you finish your water, go to bed." I said. "Yes ma'am." Jay replied.

I took the garbage bags upstairs and stuffed every piece of Jason's things and placed everything that wasn't on hangers in the bags. I took all his suits that were in the closet out and laid them across the lazy boy that was in our room. I made it easy for him, all he had to do was grab his things and go.

I glanced at the clock and it was eleven o'clock. I went and got in the shower. As the water hit my face, I realized that Jason has never valued me as being his wife. He only sees me as someone that makes him look good when we're out in public around his colleagues, church members, family, and friends. He doesn't see that I truly love him but now I'm ready to let him go. I know my worth and I refuse to sit here and let his ass disrespect me and treat me like I'm nothing. If I don't take pride in who I am and who made me to be the woman that I am today, then no one else will. "If you want to play these little games Jason, I'll play the game right along with you," I said to myself.

I dried myself off and slipped into my pajamas. It's a little chilly outside so to be all nice and warm in my PJs will be good. I walked out the bathroom as Jason was just walking through our bedroom door. He didn't say anything and neither did I at first. "Damn, you look horrible. I guess if you want to stop getting beat up, you'll stop sleeping with married or involved women." I said. "Whatever Jannice. I'm going to bed." Jason said, taking off his shoes. "Boy, I don't know where you going to bed at but you'll not going to bed here. Go sleep with one of your whores and get your ass out of my house." I said. "I'm not going anywhere." Jason said.

I think Jason thinks I'm some pushover and he can tell me what he's not going to do after his ass just got caught cheating. "Look Jason, your clothes are over there in those trash bags and your suits are all on top the recliner. So I suggest you find somewhere else to stay, otherwise I will bring our two children in here and you can tell them why you look the way you do and where were you tonight. Tell them why their father is a lying, cheating ass, pretending to be pastor, if not, then I suggest you get your shit and get the hell out of here." I said, standing up with my arms folded.

Jason realized I wasn't backing down so he gathered his clothes and started going downstairs. He made about four trips into our bedroom and as he grabbed the last three suits off the recliner, he turned and looked at me. "I'll call you before this week is over with and we can discuss what we're going to do from here on out." Jason said. "From here on out? What do you mean from here on out? You already made your decision when you lied and told me you were going to a card game at Marcus place, but instead you went to your little side chick house. But I bet you had no idea what her husband had in store for you, huh? Jason, you better stop what you're doing and then be up in the pulpit, preaching and shouting and carrying on. You better stop playing with God like that, knowing you're not real at all with how you say God called you to preach. Stop playing with God!" I said.

Jason just walked out of our room. I know Jay and Myra will be full of questions when they notice that their father isn't living here anymore. Am I ready to close this chapter in my life and walk away from it all? I am. I deserve better because I know my worth. One day I'll meet someone who will love and cherish me because Jason is definitely not it.

CHAPTER

3

On my Terms

I warmed up my lunch in the breakroom and sat down at the table. I was the only one in here so I didn't have to wait to use the microwave. I had a moment to think about all the turmoil that just happened last night, but it's nothing that God and I can't work out.

I closed my eyes and prayed over my food and my life. I started eating my lunch, when Adrienne walked in. "Hey girl." Adrienne said, as she hugged me. "Hey Adrienne. How are you?" I asked. "I'm okay. How are you? Is everything okay?" Adrienne asked. "Yes, everything is fine," I said.

Adrienne placed her food in the microwave and then sat across from me. "Come on Jannice, I know you. Are you forgetting how long we've been best friends? We've been friends for thirty years now. I know when things aren't right with you. If you don't want to tell me what's going on with you, I can respect that but don't tell me that everything is fine, because you know it's not." Adrienne said.

I know things were about to get rough for me and I needed a support group that I could count on so I decided to open up to Adrienne.

Adrienne got up and got her food from the microwave and sat back down. I told her what Jason did and I made him leave our house and that I'm in the process of filling for a divorce. "Oh Lord Jannice, I had no idea you were going through this. Why didn't you tell me? Adrienne asked. "Adrienne, what was I going to tell you that my husband screws everything that moves and thinks he's going to come back home and sleep with me and act like nothing has happened? This isn't something that you go around discussing with people." I said. "I know Jannice but I'm one of your best friends. I'm not just anybody." Adrienne said.

I know Adrienne meant well but some things you just need to figure it out yourself. You can't go around telling your business to everyone. "I know Adrienne and your right. I'm sorry I didn't tell you what was going on with me. I just had to figure this out first of what all I was going to do and how I was going to handle this," I said. "It's okay, but don't keep things bottled up inside like that Jannice, because if you do that, eventually you'll explode and trust me you don't want that," Adrienne said. "You're right. I don't," I replied.

Teresa and Tim walked in the breakroom. Teresa and Tim are two third grade teachers and the biggest gossipers at the school. The last thing I wanted was for them to have my business all over the damn school. "We'll talk later Jannice. Let me get back to my office," Adrienne said, getting up from the table with her lunch.

Adrienne doesn't care for Teresa or Tim, after she found out they went to the superintendent about smelling alcohol on her one afternoon. The superintendent did an investigation on Adrienne but since she didn't find any truth to their story, she dropped it and allowed Adrienne to come back to work. Adrienne later found out that they were the ones responsible for telling on her.

I knew Adrienne had a drinking problem after her ex-husband filed for a divorce and took their son away from her. I even noticed a few times at work that she smelled like straight up vodka but of course I would never tell on her. I pulled Adrienne aside and told her she had to get herself together before she loses her job and her son for good. Adrienne struggled for a while but eventually she got herself together. She's five years sober now and I'm extremely proud of her. She later got her son Jermaine back and living her best life now.

Adrienne said if she finds any grounds to fire Teresa and Tim, she would jump off a building to make that happen. I laughed at her comment but I told her to just focus on her sobriety and her son and God will take care of those two. Adrienne agreed and Sharese and I promised to be there for her every step of the way.

I finished my lunch, not saying anything to Teresa or Tim. They know a lot of staff here know they were behind Adrienne's suspension and we all basically stay clear from them both. I grabbed my lunch bowl and washed it out in the sink and was heading to my class when my cell phone rang.

I looked at my phone and saw that Jason was calling. I sucked my teeth but answered his call anyway, in case it was about the children. "Hello," I answered. "Hey Jannice. How are you?" Jason asked. "I'm okay. What can I do for you?" I asked, getting right to the point. "Is there any way we can meet today to talk?" Jason asked. "Why?" I asked. "I'll tell you all that if you agree to meet with me this afternoon." Jason said.

I know I shouldn't entertain Jason but I guess curiosity got the best of me. "Yes, I guess I can do that." I said. "Okay, I'll come around six o'clock, if that's okay with you?" Jason asked. "Yes. I guess that'll be fine." I said. "Good. I'll come over to the house." Jason said. "Okay, cool. I'll see you then." I said, hanging up the phone.

I just finished grading papers and was heading to my car. I made a little note that two of my male students weren't doing good in my class. I know I had to reach out to both their parents and tell them what's going on. Cameron James, one of my students that's struggling with his work doesn't seem to care much about school but he comes to school in brand new Jordan's every week. It amazes me how many of my students' parents are more concern about what they're children are wearing, instead of what they're learning. Yes, Jordan's are nice but that can't get you to knowing how to do your homework or graduating from high school.

I arrived home and sat on the couch for a few seconds before starting dinner. Myra ran up to me, giving me a big hug. "Hey Mom. How are you doing?" Myra asked. "I'm fine baby. How are you I asked. "I'm doing good. Same old, same old." Myra said, as if she has a job or something.

Jay walked in and gave me a hug as well. "Hey Mom. When did you get in?" Jay asked. "I just got in about five minutes ago," I said, as I returned his hug. "What are you about to do?" I asked. "I'm about to fix me and Myra a sandwich. Do you want one?" Jay asked. "No thank you. Just make sure you wash your hands. I'm about to start dinner shortly." I said.

I decided to go ahead and make dinner before I change my mind. I took all my ingredients out and started frying my pork chops. About thirty minutes later, everything was done and smelling so good. I wanted Jason to smell the food because smother pork chops are his favorite. Maybe I just wanted him to think about what he messed up for his little side chick. I tasted a little of the gravy on the spoon, realizing it needed just a little salt. I sprinkled a little more salt in the gravy and stirred it up, when I heard the doorbell rang.

I went to the door and peaked out the window and saw Jason standing there with a bouquet of roses in his hand. I know damn well this fool doesn't think this is going to work. It takes more than some dry ass roses to win me over.

I opened the door and let Jason inside. "Hello," I said, as he walked in. "Hey baby, these are for you" Jason said, trying to kiss me. I stepped out the way and took the roses from him before he could kiss me. "You can follow me into the kitchen," I said, putting the roses in a vase of water. "You wanted to meet?" I asked.

Jason sat down at the kitchen table while I checked on dinner. "So what is it you wanted to talk about?" I asked, turning the rice off and walking over to sit next to him. "Jannice look, I know I've made a lot of mistakes in our marriage and I know you're tired of it," Jason said. "No, I'm done," I said, with a stern face. "So you're done?" Jason asked, looking as if there was the slightest little hope for us on his face. "Yes I am. You've cheated on me for the last time. I gave you two chances and you struck out on the third. So there is no salvaging or rekindling anything here. You've made your choice and I've made mine." I said, folding my arms.

Jason tried touching my arm, as I snatched away. "So are you going to tell me what you wanted?" I asked. "Yes. I have nowhere else to go, so I need to come back home." Jason said. I burst out laughing as if Jason was a comedian or something. "Jason, why the hell didn't you think about that when you were cheating? You didn't think that if you got caught, where would you go?" I asked. "No, I didn't." Jason said, lowering his head as if he was ashamed of his actions and couldn't look at me. "Nope you didn't. You know why? You didn't think your ass would get caught did you?" I asked. Jason didn't say anything. He just looked at me with an apologetic look on his face.

I got up and stirred the rice pot, just to make sure the rice wasn't too sticky. "What are you cooking? It sure smells great in here." Jason said. "I'm making smothered pork chops in gravy and on a bed of rice." I said. "Wow, my favorite. I always love when you made that." Jason said. I just smiled at his comment. "The kids asked me to make it for them." I said lying, knowing Jason would smell the aroma when he came over and would want some.

Jason just stared at me with tears in his eyes, as if he really was sorry for what he did, or maybe it's because his ass really had nowhere else to go. "Would you like to stay for dinner? We have more than enough and besides the children would be glad to have you over." I said. "That would be great." Jason said, with a huge smile on his face.

I actually felt sorry for him, looking at his little puppy dog eyes. It was those same puppy dog eyes that made me fell in love with him twelve years ago. It was those puppy dog eyes that I looked into when we first made love for the first time. It was those same eyes that I said "I do," to when I gave him my hand in marriage and we promised to spend the rest of our lives together.

I suddenly felt a sharp pain in my heart when I realized those same puppy dog eyes were the ones I caught him in not one, not two but three affairs with three different women. He gave me that same look when he told me he would never do it again but kept doing it, over and over. Those puppy dog eyes don't mean shit to me now. There's no place for Jason in my heart or in my life anymore.

I took a deep breath and looked at him. "Look, I'll tell you what I'll do, I'll let you stay in the guest room for two weeks, until our divorce is over with and we sign the dotted line on our divorce papers. You will be in this house by six o'clock each night, with no exceptions. If you're a second pass six, the locks will be changed and you will not come back here anymore. Can you handle that?" I asked. "Six-o'clock is too early. What about eight-o'clock?" Jason asked, as if he had a choice. "No, these are my conditions you can either take it or leave it. And this agreement expires after dinner, so I'll give you until then to decide. These are my terms, so take it or leave it." I said.

Jason stood up from the table. "Okay Jannice, I'll agree with your terms. How soon can I come back?" Jason asked. "You can come back tonight if you want to." I said. "Okay, I have all my clothes in the car still so I'll bring them inside now and some after dinner." Jason said. "Okay, just remember this is only until we sign our divorce papers, so I suggest you be looking for a place as soon as possible. Because you having a place or not having a place, your ass is still getting out as soon as we sign the divorce papers. Do you understand?" I asked. "Yes I do." Jason said. "Good." I said.

Jason went outside to get his things from his car. I started smiling because I know I'm going to make this man see exactly what he lost and can never get back.

CHAPTER

4

A CLOSED DOOR

I had Myra sitting between my legs on the floor, while I fixed her hair. Myra seem to be on cloud nine since dinner today. She loves having her father around and I knew he was the reason she's been smiling. I put the last rubber band on Myra's ponytail. "All done sweetheart. Let me wrap your hair up so you'll be all set for school tomorrow." I said. "Good Mommy. I want to be pretty for school tomorrow and look just like you." Myra said. "Like me? Why you want to look just like me Myra?" I asked. "Because your beautiful Mommy," Myra said, smiling. "Thank you baby and you're just as beautiful as I am." I said.

Myra stood up and hugged me tightly. "Mommy, I love you." Myra said. "I love you too sweetheart." I said. "Mommy, can I ask you a question?" Myra asked, looking up at me with her beautiful brown eyes. "Sure sweetheart but after that, off to bed," I said. "Okay Mommy, but are you and Daddy going to get a divorce?" Myra asked. "A divorce? What do you know about a divorce? Myra, you're only five years old," I said. "Sage mom and dad are getting a divorce. Sage told me that her mom made her dad leave their house because he wouldn't help her pay the bills." Myra said.

I shook my head when Myra said that. "Well, I will tell you this sweetheart, if your Dad and I decide to separate or get a divorce, that doesn't mean we don't still love you or your brother. We'll always love you both. No matter what. You will always be my little girl and that will never change." I said. "Okay Mommy." Myra said, giving me a hug before she went off to bed.

I sat on the bed just thinking about what Myra just asked me. She and her brother knows exactly what's going on. No matter how much Jason and I try to keep this from them, they know the truth. Jason did this to our family. He chooses to leave his family for his little whores and I'm done pretending like nothing has happened. I've looked the other way far too long and I refuse to keep looking that way any longer.

I grabbed my night gown out the top drawer, along with my towel from out the bathroom. I went to my bathroom and ran the shower water. I got inside and as the water ran across my face, I wanted it to wash away the day that I first met Jason. I remember that day at my Grandfather's church, when Jason father came and preached our five-day revival. Jason walked up to me after I just finished singing my solo, "His eyes is on the Sparrow," and he complimented me on how beautiful I sounded. He told me I had such an angelic voice that demanded everyone to stop and listen to me. I believed him then and I believed every word he told me since then. No matter how much I knew he was lying, I still wanted to believe him.

I cut the shower off and dried myself off. I lotion my body down and walked in my bedroom. Jason scared the shit out of me as he stood there staring at me in my bedroom as if this was still the room we shared together. I stood there facing him, butt ass naked. This man looked me up and down as if this was his first time he's ever saw me naked before. I know he enjoyed what he saw because he licked his lips in a seductive way as if he wanted to devour my body. "Is there something you need?" I asked, not trying to cover myself up or anything. I wanted him to see how he messed up. "Yes, I just wanted to know if you had a clean towel that I could get? Jay took the last clean towel in the linen closet to take his shower." Jason said. "Sure, let me see." I said, walking over to get a clean towel out the top of the closet. "Here you go." I said, handing it to him.

Jason took the towel and stood there still staring at me. "Is there anything else you need?" I asked. "Yes, you." Jason said, walking towards me. I put my hand up to stop him before he tried to touch me or invade my personal space. "You had me but I wasn't good enough for you remember? Can you close the door on your way out please?" I asked.

The look of disappointment that displayed Jason's face was priceless. Jason finally smiled as he was about to walk out of my bedroom. "And Jason." I called out. "Yes." Jason replied. "Can you please knock the next time you need something instead of you just coming into my bedroom. That way, I can be fully dressed when you walk in." I said. Jason nodded his head and walked out.

I went over and locked my bedroom door. I wanted to burst out laughing because if looks could kill, I would be laying on my bedroom floor right about now. I swear I'm going to enjoy torturing this man and making him think twice about ever cheating on me in the first place.

CHAPTER

5

Wine & Dine

Adrienne invited both Sharese and myself over to her place for "wine and dine." We usually try to do one every first of the month, depending on how busy we are, if we even have one for that month. We sometimes have two a month, if we just need to unwind, wine and dine. I love wine and dine because it gives us a chance to see each other, eat good and get our drink on, while we talk about all the shit that's going on in our lives, as far as our children or our relationships or lack of one.

Adrienne and Sharese know that Jason and I are separated, they just don't know I allowed him back into our house. I know they will both think I'm crazy but hell, it's not like they haven't made some dumb, crazy decisions in their lives as well.

I stopped at Publix and grabbed a bottle of wine, along with some chips and salsa. We don't go all out with food or anything. Whoever host it, normally buy a fruit tray, and make some wings and some kind of salad, and of course the wine all three of us have to buy a bottle. Adrienne only drinks one glass but we told her, she doesn't have to do that just to satisfy us, I'm fine with drinking all the damn wine all by myself. She laughed and said, one glass won't hurt anything. With our wine and dine it can get a little off the chain that, we have to call an uber to get back home.

I left Publix and was heading over to Adrienne's house. I told the kids that I would be home a little later, and I told Jason as well, only because he needed to be there with the kids. Jason's crazy ass had the audacity to ask me where I was going. I looked at him like he had lost his damn mind or something. I told him he has lost that right to ask me a question like that. He didn't say anything but stretched his eyes. I was going to tell him I'm going over to Adrienne's house with Sharese and he won't find me entertaining the opposite sex or being thrown out no one's house, but I didn't say it.

Jason told me to enjoy myself and that he'll take care of the kids. I'm actually pleasantly shocked because all before, he never made time for the kids, he always put that off on me. I guess that can change when you have nowhere else to go and you have to change things up some.

I pulled up at Adrienne's house and knocked on the door. I see Sharese isn't here yet, but it's only five-forty-five. Adrienne greeted me at the door. "Hey Jannie. Good to see you. Come on in." Adrienne said, as she hugged me and took the bag from me to the kitchen.

I walked in the den behind Adrienne and sat in the lazy-boy chair. Adrienne has a nice three-bedroom condominium by the lake. She moved here shortly after her divorce. She knew this place was more in her budget. She knew she couldn't afford to live in their old house alone, so they sold it and split the proceeds. "You're a little early." Adrienne yelled from the kitchen. "I know, I was afraid if I sat down at home, then I definitely wouldn't be coming back out. You know how we get when we get home and all comfortable on the couch." I said. "That's so true. Do you need help in the kitchen?" I asked. "No, not really. The wings have about ten more minutes to go and they'll be ready." Adrienne said. "Okay." I said.

Adrienne came in the den and sat down. "How are you Jannice? You look a little tired," Adrienne said. "No, I'm actually good," I said. "That's good. I'm glad you didn't let Jason and the separation tore you down." Adrienne said. I wanted to tell her that I let Jason moved back in our house but I figured, I'll wait until Sharese gets here, that way I won't have to repeat myself.

I heard a car door slam and Adrienne went to the window. "Sharese is here," Adrienne said, as she went to the door. "Oh okay." I replied. Sharese walked in and greeted us both and gave Adrienne a bag. "Hey girl. How was your day?" I asked. "It was okay and quite boring. I swear I need to do something to occupy my time outside of work." Sharese said. "Like what, going to the gym or something?" I asked. "No, I don't feel that damn good." Sharese said. Adrienne and I burst out laughing. "Yall, I'm going to take the wings out the oven and then everything will be ready." Adrienne said. "Sounds good." Sharese said.

Sharese is a plant supervisor at Cooper Tools. She's been there for seventeen years, since we graduated. She works first shift and put herself through college. As soon as Sharese got her bachelor's degree in business, the company promoted her as a supervisor.

Most people will never understand the friendship I have with these two. Sharese and I were born friends when we came out the womb. Whenever I tell people how we met, they couldn't believe it. Sharese's mom and my mother met the day they were about to give birth to us. Sharese and I are our parents first child. My mother told me that Sharese's mom Julia who I now call Aunt Julia, and her were both afraid since they never gave birth before so they bonded and became the best of friends that day. They both went in the delivery room together. Mom said back then it was two in a room, which was divided by a long curtain. Aunt Julia gave birth to Sharese at six-thirty-five that morning and my mom gave birth to me at six-forty that morning. We're exactly five minutes apart. When we tell people that we were friends at birth, that's exactly what we mean.

Sharese and I had every single birthday party together growing up, until I got married ten years ago. I knew deep down Sharese was happy for me but she felt that Jason was replacing her in my life. She finally understood that I was married and needed to celebrate my birthday with my husband and later my family, after my children were born.

I remember one day Sharese and I were playing in the park near our school and this little girl around our age came up to us and was just staring at us. We knew the girl was from our school and was in the first grade as us, because we've seen her many times before just staring at us like she had a problem. I thought the girl was a little off at first by the way she would just stand there smiling and looking. Sharese being the little bad ass that she is ask the girl what was she staring at. The girl pointed at us both and said she wanted to be our friend and she walked over to us and hugged us both and told us her name was Adrienne. Sharese told Adrienne she could be our friend but I was her very best friend and as long as she didn't try to be closer to her than me, and the other way around with me with her, then we all could be friends. Adrienne nodded her head and said she wanted to be best friends with both of us and not just one. These two have been here my entire life and I would kill for either one of them and I know they feel the same way about me as well. My girls and I have been friends for over thirty years and I wouldn't trade them for nothing in the world.

We've been there for each other through the darkest and happiest times of our lives. They were both in my wedding and there for the birth of my children. Sharese and I were there through Adrienne's horrible divorce and her alcohol addiction and how we prayed to God that Adrienne would get back to normal and get her son and life back together, which she did.

Adrienne and I have been there for Sharese when her father was murdered at a gas station, when someone tried to steal his car and he refuse to give it to him and when she was diagnosed with breast cancer five years ago. Lord the tears we cried during those days of how we watched Sharese lose fifty pounds and the chemo took all her hair out. I remember how we spent nights at her house and how the medication made her vomit all the times and how Sharese would cry in the tub, praying to God to just go ahead and take her on home because she couldn't take the pain. I'm glad I know a God that when the doctors had given up on Sharese, God didn't give up on her and neither did we.

The painful nights we would pace back and forth crying and praying that God would help heal my best friend and when she ranged the bell at the hospital after finishing her last day of chemo and radiation, she grabbed both Adrienne and my hand and said "yall we made it, and I couldn't have done it without God and my two best friends." The screams and the shouting that went on at that moment, it was nobody but God that did that. You would've thought the nurses, Adrienne and I were in church the way we gave God the praise for bringing my friend through and sparing her life. We knew that only death would take us away from each other because cancer couldn't do it. Our faith and prayers kept us together to this day and it was going to take us all the way through the end.

We ate and drank until our hearts was content and I was waiting for one of them to ask about Jason and was I still filing for a divorce. I knew it was coming, I could see it on the tip of their tongues. "So have you made up in your mind if you're going to file for divorce yet?" Sharese asked. "Yes, I am. It's a done deal. I'm ready to move on with my life." I said. "Are you really?" Adrienne asked. "Yes. I've gave Jason chance after chance and now I'm done. You know he's trying to act all lovey, dovey now." I said. "Hmm, it's a little too late for all that now. Where is he living or do you even know?" Sharese asked.

I wanted to change the subject but I knew all along this was going to come up. "He's staying back at the house." I said. "Wait! Didn't you tell us you put him out?" Adrienne asked. "Yes, but he came asking can he at least come back because he doesn't have anywhere else to go." I said. "Shit. His ass should've thought about that before he did what the hell he did." Sharese said. "Damn right." Adrienne chimed in.

They were both right and I know they were looking at me sideways when I told them that. "Well you guys look, he is the father of my children. I didn't want to see him on the street." I said. "Well, I guess you're right, but I would've told him to go back and stay with his little whores that I caught him with but I guess he can't stay with her since the tramp is married." Sharese said, rolling her eyes. "Yall, he is staying in the guestroom. I told him he could stay in the guestroom until he finds an apartment or until we sign the divorce papers. So if he knows what I know, his ass better be looking for his own place. And besides that I want Jason to see that I'm moving on with my life. I want him to see how he messed up what he had." I said. "So you want him to see you're not moping around the house looking all sad huh? And living your best life right?" Adrienne asked. "Damn right." I said. "And you should." Adrienne and Sharese said at the same time.

CHAPTER

6

Temptation

I just got home around nine o'clock from our "wine and dine" with my girls. I walked in Jay's room and he was just getting in the bed. "Hey sweetheart. Did you have a good day?" I asked. "I did Mom. How was yours?" Jay asked. "It was good. I had a great time with your two aunties and they told me to tell you hello." I said. "Okay." Jay said, looking a little tired. "You look tired baby." I said. "I am Mom. I'm going to sleep now so goodnight and I love you." Jay said. "I love you too son and goodnight." I replied, closing his bedroom door.

I went to Myra's room to check on her. Hopefully she was in the bed this time of night. Myra door was cracked and she was kneeling on the floor praying.

"Dear God,

Thank you for waking me up this morning and allowing me to have a wonderful day. I thank you for my two best friends Sage, and Riley. Thank you for all my teachers and my aunts, uncles, and my cousins. Thank you for my Grandparents, my brother Jay and my mom and dad. Thank you for letting my daddy come back home. I know my daddy and mom are mad at each other but please Lord, don't let them get a divorce. Jay and I both love them and we want our mom and dad to stay together so they can love us like we love them. "Thank you God. Amen." Myra said, getting off the floor and getting into bed.

I closed Myra's door and just stood there. My daughter really wants Jason and I to stay together. I wish that Jason didn't do what he did and we could get pass it but this time I can't. I think I can eventually forgive him but right now I can't. Why couldn't the love of his wife and children be enough for him to get back in his car and come back home. Why couldn't Jason realize how much I love him, and how much he loved me for him to not get involved with that married woman. I bet his ass hasn't even talked to that lady again since that night. Why would someone risk losing everything for a night of sex?

I went to my bedroom to get ready for my shower. I took off my clothes, only keeping on my bra and panties. I thought I heard the shower water running in my bathroom but wasn't sure. I know I'm not that tired that I'm imagining things. I opened my bathroom door and realized it was my shower water running. Jason was in my shower. What the hell is he doing in my shower? Why didn't he just use the one down the hallway that the kids use? Jason isn't respecting my boundaries. He can't just go in my room and use my shower when he gets ready to. We're going to have to talk about this. He's making me regret allowing him to come back home.

I went back in the bathroom and tap on the shower door. Jason jumped, as if I scared him. "Hey Jannice. I'm sorry I didn't know you were home." Jason said. "Okay Jason. Why are you showering in my bathroom? Why didn't you just use the shower down the hallway?" I asked. "Because both of the children had to shower for bed and since you were out, I just went ahead and use our shower in here. I'm sorry to have intruded," Jason said. "Okay. I rather you just use the one down the hall though." I said. "Okay, I'll use that one from now on," Jason said. "Thank you," I replied, walking out the bathroom.

I took my robe off the chair and covered myself up. I didn't want Jason to have any ideas that we're about to have sex or anything. I heard the shower water stop and minutes later I heard the bathroom door open as well.

I turned to my right so I wouldn't see when Jason comes out the bathroom, because I know his ass is going to try something. He's on a mission to try and win me over but that will never happen. Once I say I'm done with you, I'm done. I heard Jason walking around in our bedroom on the hardwood floors. Why can't he just get his ass out of here so I can take my shower and get some sleep.

I tried keeping my eyes close, until Jason close my bedroom door but he never did. I felt his footsteps coming closer and closer towards me. What the hell is Jason up to? "Jannice. Jannice." Jason called out to me. I opened my eyes, like I was asleep. Jason was standing in front of me butt ass naked, holding his dick in his hand.

Any other time, I would've jump straight on top of him and submit myself to him but now things were different. I had no interest in doing anything sexual with him. Any feelings or desire I had for him has went out the door, since I know he's around here giving out community dick to the entire community. Jason leaned over and tried to kiss me and I pushed him a way. "What are you doing?" I asked, as he stepped back. "I'm trying to make love to you if you'll let me." Jason said. "Jason, please leave me alone," I said. "You don't want to make love?" Jason asked, with a cocky smile on his face. "Hell no! Because you're out there sleeping with anything that moves. You think I'm going to put my life in jeopardy, sleeping with you? Hell no Jason. I'm the mother of your children and that's it. We are still technically married but that's only on paper. You stepped out our marriage a long time ago. I've never been with anyone else since I met you and definitely since I married you, but you can't say the same came you? Please put something on and go back to the guestroom. I will tell you one more time that I'm done with you and I mean that," I said.

Jason put some pajama pants on and walked out my room. Lord I'm so damn horny and right now I could use my husband in here with me but oh well. I guess I'll use my little toy that's in my plastic box under my bed. I took out my toy and turned it on. This is a damn shame that I trust this vibrator more then I trust my own husband. I don't have to worry about this thing giving me any STD's or anything that penicillin and a shot can't cure.

If I was to give Jason another chance he would be back to his old self again next week or next month, back to his cheating ways again. There's no telling how many affairs he's actually had on me. I know of three but who knows, it's probably so many that even he can't keep track with.

I'm not one of these women that will let their husband do whatever and whoever he wants and think I'm going to be right here waiting for him to come home. I don't know why he can't come to grips that it's over with and there's nothing he can do about it at this point. Grandma always said "you made that bed, now you have to lie in it."

CHAPTER

7

I'm not Pretending

My alarm started blasting at nine o'clock this morning. I got up and took my shower and through on some sweatpants and a tee-shirt. I walked in the kitchen and Jason had made breakfast. He made grits, eggs, bacon and toast. Man this dude is really on a roll. The kids were sitting at the table eating. "Good morning." I said, kissing both Jay and Myra on the cheek. "Good morning Mom." Jay and Myra replied. "Good morning beautiful," Jason said. I just smiled, because I definitely didn't want to cause a scene at breakfast and ruin it for the kids. "Mom, you didn't kiss Daddy this morning." Myra said, looking at me with her beautiful brown big eyes. "How about I kiss all up on you." I said, getting up and kissing all over Myra's face. "Okay Mommy, that's enough kisses," Myra said, smiling.

Myra and Jay were just about finished with their breakfast. "Jannice your breakfast is in the microwave if you want any," Jason said. I hesitated at first if I should eat what he made but I don't think he's that damn crazy to try and poison me or anything.

I smiled, knowing not even Jason is that cruel and evil to do something like that. I went and took my food out the microwave and sat at the table to eat. Myra and Jay just finished eating and they put their plates in the sink. "Myra and Jay go ahead and take your clothes out for church and I'll be there to help you shortly." Jason said. "Okay Daddy," they said, heading upstairs.

Jason stood up and put his plate and glass in the sink. He washed the dishes and wiped off the countertops and table. I couldn't help from smiling to myself because these were things I could never get him to do before and now that he's trying to win me back, he's pulling all kinds of tricks out the bag. "I'm afraid it's just a little too late for that now Jason." I mumbled to myself.

I finished eating and I went over to wash my plate and glass out. "I got it." Jason said. "Okay," I replied, not getting an argument out of me. I went to the den and turned on the TV. I started watching Joyce Myers. I love the way she preaches and teach the word of God. Jason walked in the den. "Jannice, are you going to church this morning?" Jason asked. "No I'm not." I said. "May I ask why?" Jason asked.

I looked at him with the nastiest look on my face, as if I was about to go the hell off, but I tried to compose myself the best I could. "Because I will not stand by your side at church, as if we're some happy little church family and that I'm the loving first lady to my supporting husband. I'm not pretending for you or anyone else. You might be okay with getting on the pulpit preaching your heart out, knowing damn well it's not coming from anywhere. There's no telling how many people you've slept with in our congregation. I've looked like Bo Bo the clown for far too long, and I refuse to do it any longer," I said.

Jason just stood there looking at me, as if I lost my mind or something because I'm not willing to pretend that we're some happy little family. "Jannice, what will our members think about the first lady not coming to church?" Jason asked. Before I knew it I burst out laughing. "Jason I can give two rats ass what the members think why I'm not coming back to church. I refuse to walk up in there while you're still preaching. All you are is a damn devil in a robe, pretending to be something you're not. But I guess it's easier for you than it is for me since you've been pretending for a long time now. You've been pretending to love me and that your happy and being faithful in our marriage and you know that's a damn lie. So you go ahead and put on your robe and do your best pastoring performance on stage, because Lord knows you do that so well," I said.

Jason sucked his teeth and headed upstairs. "Jason," I called out to him. "Yes," he answered as he stopped walking and turned to look at me. "You better be careful how you're playing with God like that. The bible speaks of false prophets and you read what happened to them. Keep playing with God and the word. He will show you exactly who he is." I said. Jason didn't say anything else. He just stormed off like a five-year boy, stomping upstairs after being told "no."

I finished watching Joyce Myers morning service and then I turned the TV off. I headed upstairs to help Myra get ready for church. Even though I wasn't going, I would never stop the children from going.

I knocked on Myra's door. "Come in?" Myra replied. "Hey sweetie, do you need any help getting ready for church?" I asked. "Not really Mommy but you can stay if you want to and talk to me." Myra said. I just smiled at my little princess sounding so grown. "I sure will. So show me what you're going to wear?" I asked.

Myra pulled out a royal blue and white dress and placed it on the bed. "Mom, what do you think about this one?" Myra asked. "Now that's a great choice Myra. You're going to look beautiful in this dress." I said, holding it up. "Thanks Mom. You know you should wear your royal blue dress too, so that way we can be dressed alike and be twins." Myra said, smiling.

I know I'm going to have to hear a ton of questions when I tell Myra that I'm not going to church with them, so I might as well get it over with now. "Sweetie, I'm not going to church this morning," I said. "Why Mom? We always go to church together as a family," Myra said. "I know baby, but things have changed. You and your brother are the most important people in my life and I love you two unconditionally. Myra, things are going to change for our family and it's okay. Just know that you and your brother mean everything to your father and I. Okay?" I said. "Okay Mom." Myra replied. "Well, I'll let you get dress and if you need me to brush your hair back, just let me know." I said. "I will Mom." Myra said, as she picked up her dress off the bed.

I closed the door behind me and pressed my head on Myra's bedroom door. My children are my world and I'll do anything for them except stay with their father just to keep us all together. I've done that too long as it is. I think Jay and Myra will be okay when the divorce is final. I took a week before starting to file my divorce, just to make sure this is really what I want and it is. I guess I needed to decide if our marriage was worth saving and I know now it's not. There's just no way I can keep turning the other cheek after he keeps slapping me in the face with his many affairs.

Once the love is gone between two people because of cheating, it's hard to get that love and trust back. Jason wants me to walk in our church and smile and greet the members, like we're so in love and that we have a perfect marriage but that would be the farthest thing from the truth. I refuse to pretend that we're happy when I know we're not and we have just as much problems as any other married couple in our church. No, I'm done pretending with his fake ass.

CHAPTER

8

Ricardo James

I pulled up at work about fifteen minutes early, which is a little unusual for me. The earliest I've ever gotten to work was five minutes, which is just enough time for me to park and walk inside. I wonder if Adrienne is here already? She's probably in her office having her morning coffee.

I passed her office and saw her holding up her cup to drink. I went and knocked on the wall before just walking inside her office. "Come in girl," Adrienne said, as I closed the door behind me. I hugged Adrienne and then sat down. I've been here teaching for over twelve years and Adrienne and I have always kept our friendship on hush, hush. We both agreed that no one needed to know that we're been besties since the first grade. You know gossipers and we definitely don't want people thinking that she gives me special treatment since we're friends.

"How are you bestie?" Adrienne asked. "I'm doing okay but I wanted to know do you still have the divorce lawyer information that you hired to handle your divorce?" I asked. "Yes I do." Adrienne said, as she started looking through her phone contacts. Adrienne grabbed a sticky off the top of her desk and wrote the information down for me. "Her name is Desiree

Spencer. Trust me she'll get you what you deserve and some. So I guess you're ready to do this huh?" Adrienne asked. "Yes, I am. I think deep down this is what I need. I'm not the type to just sit around knowing my husband is cheating on me and I'm just staying with him. No I'm going to free him and myself," I said.

Adrienne got up and high five me. "Shit, I know that's right. There's nothing like walking around in your own peace, but knowing deep down you tried to make it work but it just didn't. Trust me, Jason is going to realize what he let go and he's going to get exactly what he deserves. They always do," Adrienne said. "That's the truth." I said, standing up from my seat, when I saw Mrs. Nancy the secretary walked in and sat at her desk. Adrienne and I shook hands like two professional women that just had a little chat with each other.

I grabbed my bag off the floor and was walking out Adrienne's office. "Jannice, don't forget we have a PTA meeting today at six." Adrienne said. "Oh dang, I totally forgot all about that. I'll be right here." I said. "Good." Adrienne replied, as she waved at me.

I walked to my classroom mad that I had that PTA meeting this afternoon. I wanted to see if I could meet Ms. Spencer and discuss my divorce with her, but now that's been cancelled. I guess I can go tomorrow after work instead. I know I need to do this as soon as possible before Jason thinks I've changed my mind about filing for one.

I went to McDonalds and grabbed a big mac, since I'll be at school the entire day and partially tonight as well. I definitely didn't want to be talking to any of the parents and my stomach starts growling or anything.

I had about eight parents that showed up to the PTA meeting which is more then I usually have. Normally I have about four parents that come out so tonight was a pleasant surprise.

I sat down in the cafeteria looking around in case a parent comes in asking for me. I waited and it's been about thirty minutes since I had another parent. I was about to leave when this medium height, dark-skinned man, with dreads walked in. One of the teachers pointed to me and the man started walking over towards me.

The man was extremely handsome with a dark chocolate skin tone. His dreads came past his shoulders and were nice and neatly trimmed. "Hello, I'm Ricardo James. I'm Cameron James uncle. Cameron's parents had to work so they asked me to step in for them tonight." Mr. James said as we shook hands. "Mr. James, so nice to meet you. I'm Cameron's teacher Mrs. Jannice Davis." I said. "So nice to meet you Mrs. Davis." Mr. James replied. "You as well." I replied.

Mr. James and I sat down to talk. "Mr. James, Cameron is struggling a little in my class. He doesn't turn in his homework and he's not doing good on any of his test. I tried calling his parents but I haven't got any return phone calls." I said. "Mrs. Davis, I'm so sorry for my sister and brother-in-law lack of communication but I'll do whatever I can to help Cameron and that includes whipping his behind too." Mr. James said.

I smiled at Mr. James comment. "Mr. James, I think Cameron just need someone to push him and make sure he does what he needs to do on his homework assignments. Cameron is a very bright student, he just need that extra push, like a lot of students do," I said. "Oh I'll push him alright," Mr. James said.

Mr. James, sounds like he's really invested in Cameron's education but I just hope Cameron is as well. Mr. James kept addressing me with his eyes and I must admit that Mr. Ricardo James is definitely an attractive man. Chocolate has always been my weakness in the guys I've dated but Jason is brown-skinned. Maybe if I stayed with the chocolate brothers, I wouldn't be going through the shit I'm going through off Jason ass now.

Mr. James has to be around one hundred and eighty pounds. He has a muscular body tone and his dreads has to be the best well-groomed dreads I've ever seen on a man before. I was so mesmerized by Ricardo handsome ass that I didn't realize he was asking me something, until he hit the top of the table. I jumped at the sound of the hard noise. "I'm sorry Mrs. Davis, I didn't mean to scare you," Mr. James said. "It's okay, I started daydreaming for a second," I said. "Mr. James, started smiling, as if he knew my thoughts were about him, which he would be correct. "Mrs. Davis, do you think that Cameron can benefit from some tutoring on the side?" Mr. James asked. "Yes Mr. James, I think that will help tremendously." I said.

Mr. James started laughing. "What's so funny?" I asked. "You are. I'm just not use to be called Mr. James. You're calling me that like I'm a sixty-year-old man or something. I'm only thirty-six years old, which is probably a few years older than you. Please call me Ricardo," Ricardo said.

"I'm sorry, I didn't mean to offend you. I just didn't know. Some people like to be all formal. I didn't want to call you by your first name until you gave me permission to do so. And to answer your question, I'm thirty five. I'll be turning thirty-six in a few months." I said. "Oh nice. I bet your husband has something nice planned for you." Ricardo said.

I laughed at Ricardo's sly way of asking me if I was married. "I seriously doubt that. He probably will be out taking his other lady out on my birthday. We're currently going through a divorce." I said. "Wow." Ricardo said, in disbelief. I wonder why he said that. "Why did you say wow?" I asked. "Because it's hard to believe he's about to let a beautiful woman like you go. I swear if you were mine, I would fight tooth and nails to persuade you not to leave me and always make you feel like a beautiful queen that you are." Ricardo said.

I know damn well Ricardo James isn't flirting with me in this cafeteria and at a PTA meeting. I couldn't help from cheesing from ear to ear for the beautiful compliment. "Well he has. I guess some men don't know a good loyal woman when they see one. They rather run behind the trash in the street, when they have a good woman at home." I said. "You're right. Some men don't value that, but trust me when I say I do." Ricardo said, smiling. "You better stop that Ricardo. You going to make a sister think you're flirting with her." I said. "Maybe I am." Ricardo said, as he winked his eye at me.

I happened to look down at my watch and saw it was five minutes to eight. "Ricardo, I swear you probably have a ton of women and that's probably one of your lines, you tell all of them." I said, gathering all my belongings. "Jannice, I don't have a ton of women. One woman is more than enough for me and all I need. I'm not like these other men out here, that don't know they have a good thing until It's gone. "Ricardo said. "Okay, Mr. Smooth talker. Do you mind walking me to my car?" I asked. "Sure thing. I can't have anything happening to you, especially since I haven't asked you out yet." Ricardo said.

I looked at him as he stood up and rolled my eyes. "What's that rolling your eyes for?" Ricardo asked. "You don't want to ask me out, besides I come with baggage until my divorce is final." I said. "Have you filed for divorce yet?" Ricardo asked. "No. I was going to go today until I found out we were having this PTA meeting tonight, so I'll have to go tomorrow as soon as I get off from work." I said. "So you don't want to start chatting with anyone until your divorce is final, in case you change your mind and give your husband another chance?" Ricardo asked. "No. Trust me, there is no other chances with me. I gave him two chances and his last chance, was when he struck out and he lost big time. He's trying to get me back but he knows I'm done. And trust me, when a woman is fed up, there's nothing you can do about it. I'm all the way done." I said.

Ricardo, reached down and opened my car door for me to get in. He asked for my phone. Without thinking much about it, I unlocked it and gave it to him. He put his phone number in my phone under "Rick." "Jannice, even if this is our last time talking, please don't think all men are the same because, we're not and believe me, I come with a little baggage as well. Everyone does. If you want a friend or someone to talk to than use the number. If you feel that you need to wait for a while before you can move on, I'll totally understand." Ricardo said.

I looked at Ricardo a little strange and stretched my eyes. "You come with baggage as well?" What kind of baggage do you come with?" I asked. "Well, I'll save that for our first time hanging out to tell you all of that. It's no need to tell you my life story if you're not going to be around to at least start the book." Ricardo said. "Wow, I like your little metaphor. And I except that. Well, I have your number maybe I'll reach out." I said. Ricardo had a big smile on his face. "I swear Mrs. Jannice Davis, you really intrigue me and I would love to get to know you on a personal level." Ricardo said. "We'll see Ricardo. We will see," I said, as I put my Honda in reverse and drove off, waving at him one last time.

As I drove off, I couldn't help but to smile. "Yes, Ricardo James, you intrigue me as well."

CHAPTER

9

The Divorce Papers

I just got off work and pulled up to the law office of Desiree Spencer. I made an appointment as soon as her office opened. The receptionist Laura told me she could fit me in when I get off at five this afternoon. I told Adrienne what was going on and she told me to go ahead and handle my business. That's one thing I love about working for your best friend, it comes with some perps. I try to never take advantage so she'll think I'm just trying to be taking off work.

I got out my Honda and checked in. The receptionist told me to have a seat and Ms. Spencer will come upfront to get me. I did as I was instructed to. I took out my phone and I saw that Ricardo texted me. He's been quite consisted with texting me back and forth. I must say, "mama always said, don't go looking for a man, let them find you." The bible speaks of that as well. So the next man I meet will have to find me, because I'm definitely not going out there looking for him. Who knows maybe Ricardo could be my Boaz after all, but right now I'll settle for my knight and shining armor. Ricardo texted me asking how was my day going? I replied back telling him I was at my divorce lawyer office and I'll hit him back after

I'm done. Ricardo asked is this really what I want to do? I got a little annoyed by that text. "Hell yeah. That's why I'm here." I replied, as if he had something to do with my decision, which he didn't at all. I'm walking out of this marriage, just like Jason walked out a long time ago, while he was having his numerous affairs.

Ricardo, must have sense my aggravation with his last text. He stated, "I'm sorry about what I just said, because apparently you are sure about it if you're at a divorce lawyer's office. Sometimes I put my foot in my own mouth and don't know what to say. My mom has always told me that." Ricardo replied. I replied, telling him it wasn't a big deal and that it was okay.

I just finished sending the text when I heard my name being called. I looked up to head back and was definitely surprised that Desiree Spencer is a white lady. With a name like Desiree, I just knew she was black. "Hello, how are you Mrs. Davis?" Ms. Spencer asked. "I'll be better once this is over with." I said. "I can only imagine." Ms. Spencer said.

I followed Ms. Spencer back to her office. "Mrs. Davis, we don't have to be so formal. Please call me Rae and is it okay that I call you Jannice?" Rae asked. "that's fine." I said. "Well good. So have a seat please. So you want to file for a divorce correct?" Rae asked. "Yes that's correct," I said. "Well do you think that you two can work this out at all?" Rae asked. "No ma'am. After three affairs, trust me he struck all the way out as far as I'm concern." I said. "Damn three times. Girl, at least you tried. Shit, I would've been ready to bounce after the first one. And Jannice, I had to ask that question. That's something that the state requires us to ask all clients. I think it's stupid but I did ask." Rae said.

Talking and laughing with Rae, definitely made this divorce thing a whole lot easier. "Jannice, how long have you been married to your husband?" Rae asked. "Ten years and with two children." I said. "Do you have any proof he's been cheating?" Rae asked. "Yes, an outside child that he doesn't think I know about, as well as the pictures of his car at his last mistress house. I also have pictures with him in his underwear, while the husband whipped his ass." I said. "Jannice, how do you know about the woman he had the child with?" Rae asked. "Because the woman wanted me to leave Jason so she could have him and I refuse to then. She and I met somewhere and she told me that her son Tyler was my husband's son. I looked at little Tyler and I knew he was indeed my husband's son." I said.

Rae shook her head. "Wow, is all I can say. Do you know how to reach this woman if I need to get in touch with her?" Rae asked. "Yes, I do. The lady even gave me a DNA test as well, I guess she wanted me to see proof that she wasn't lying. I even have an eye witness with the husband that beat Jason down a week and a half ago after he caught him with his wife. I'm sure he'll testify." I said. I think the son he had from another woman is more than enough to make things go our way. So tell me what are you seeking?" Desiree asked. "I want seven thousand a month for child support for my children as well as alimony. I want him to pay for your legal fees as well." I said.

Rae jotted down something on a notepad. "Jannice, does he make that much a month? I mean he still has to live to." Rae said. "Well Jason gets six thousand each week for being the pastor and he gets an additional thirty-five hundred dollars every two weeks from his full-time job. Does that sound about right to you?" I asked.

Rae stood up and went to her file cabinet and pulled out some forms. "You do want the house right?" Rae asked. "Yes." I replied. "Okay, so we'll put this in the agreement that you keep the house and you're asking for thirteen thousand dollars each month for child support and alimony. Mr. Davis will pay for my legal fees as well." Rae said. "Yes, that sounds good. Please put in the settlement that he will maintain all health and dental insurance for the children until they are out of school as well." I said. "Okay, I'll do that." Rae replied. "Rae, do you think I can get that much each month?" I asked. "Sure I do. If we're asking for thirteen-thousand each month, that still leave him eighteen thousand to live off of, which is more than enough for him to survive on." Rae said.

I knew Jason wouldn't be please by what I'm asking for but he can't think that what he did wouldn't bring consequences. He shouldn't be too upset since I'm not asking for any of his on-line broadcast he does each Sunday morning. That's an extra two thousand each week as well but I didn't throw that in. I'll be okay with thirteen-thousand each month. I want this divorce to hit him hard and let him see that I mean business.

Rae stood up and went over to her printer. "Jannice, I'm printing out a copy of your divorce papers and a copy of our contract agreement. My fee is five thousand dollars." Rae said. I thought that was a bit high to just have two people sign some papers in front of two lawyers and say it's done and we go our own separate ways. "Oh well, this is her price and I'm not the one that has to pay her.

Rae handed me the papers and I looked over everything and then signed it. "Jannice, this is your copy to get your husband to sign it. Please inform him that just because he doesn't sign the divorce papers, doesn't mean the divorce will not stand. "Rae said. "I will." I said. "Okay, well as soon as you get him to sign the papers, bring them back to me. I'll get you both in here a long with his lawyer so we can finalize your divorce for good. How does that sound?" Rae asked. "Sounds good to me. I'm just ready to move on with my life and be done with Jason all together." I said. "Jannice, as long as you have two children, you won't be completely done with him anytime soon." Rae said. "You're right but as far as being married to him, I will be," I replied. "Yes. That's right, you'll no longer be married to him, you're correct," Rae said.

I stood from my chair and took my set of papers from Rae. I extended my hand towards her. "Thank you so much for helping me Rae. I look forward to working with you." I said. "Same here and it was a pleasure meeting you as well." Rae said.

I walked to my car and sat the papers on the passenger seat. This will be one of the hardest things I'll have to do is explain to my children that Jason and I are getting a divorce and we'll be living separately. Jay will be able to understand this a little more than Myra but I'm not looking for either one of them to take it easy. "Lord, Jason why couldn't you have done right by me and we wouldn't have to be putting our children and church members in this mess you created."

CHAPTER

10

As A Family

I walked in the house and Jason was preparing dinner. Wow, I could never get this man to cook in the entire ten years of our marriage and now he wants to cook breakfast and dinner all of a sudden. I swear the things men do when they think they already lost, to try and win you back. Shit, if he was spending more time cooking instead of sticking everything, then maybe I wouldn't be filing for a divorce.

I must admit the aroma smells amazing though. "Hey. How are you?" I asked, walking in the kitchen. "Hey pretty lady." Jason said, walking up to me to give me a hug. I stepped back and held out my hand to shake his hand. Jason gave me a crazy look but he shook my hand. "Dang, I can't even get a hug." Jason said. I just smiled only because the kids were sitting at the table doing their homework.

I walked over to greet the kids. "Hey my handsome son and beautiful daughter," I said, giving them both hugs and a kiss on the cheek. "Hey Mom, they both said together. Did you both have a good day in school?" I asked, sitting beside Myra. "It was okay Mommy. Today I was the line leader for class the entire day." Myra said. "Oh that's great baby. I bet you were the best line leader too." I said. "I did good Mommy." Myra said, smiling. "What about you Jay? How was your day?" I asked. "Well I got a "B" on my spelling test today." Jay said. "Well that's good son." I said. "Mom, that's not good. I have to study a little harder next time. I should've got an "A." Jay said, sounding disappointed. "That's okay son. You'll get an "A" next time." I said. "I sure am," Jay replied.

I'm so proud of my children. They both love school and want to always push themselves to make the best grades they can and that just thrills my heart. I wish all my third graders felt that way but clearly they don't.

Jason looked like he was about done making dinner. "Jason, what are you cooking?" I asked. "I made chicken alfredo, chef salad, garlic bread and a strawberry cheesecake. Everything is finally done so Myra and Jay, go wash your hands so you can eat." Jason said. "That sounds good." I said. "Thank you. I just hope it taste good," Jason said, with a smile.

I washed my hands after the kids sat down at the table. Jason fixed everyone's food and brought it to the table. He poured our drinks and then sat at the table across from me. "Let us join hands please." Jason said, as he said grace. I listened as he thanked God for blessing us with our dinner. His blessing was sincere and genuine. It felt like he really meant every word that came out his mouth.

We ate dinner, engaging in a little conversation here and there. "How was your day Jannice?" Jason asked. "It was great. I had an important meeting today." I said. "Oh okay. I hope everything's okay?" Jason asked. "Yes, everything will be fine," I said. I wanted to tell Jason the truth that I spoke to a lawyer today but I didn't want to ruin dinner so I decided to wait until after dinner to discuss everything with him.

Dinner was absolutely perfect. Jason did an excellent job making it. Jay and Myra looked like they were about to pop, because I certainly felt that way. "Mom, may I be excused?" Jay asked. "Yes you may," I replied. "Mom, may I be excused?" Myra asked. "Sure baby," I replied. "Thanks Dad for dinner. It was really good. I wish you cook more often instead of letting Mom do it all the time." Jay said, putting his items in the sink.

I walked over to the sink and started doing the dishes. "Thank you again for dinner Jason. Everything was delicious." I said again. "Thank you and I'm glad you enjoyed it." Jason said, as he brought his things to the sink. I finished washing everything and put the leftovers in a bowl and put it in the fridge. Jason sat down at the dinner table, as if he was waiting for me to finish washing the dishes. I dried my hands off and grabbed the envelope with my divorce papers inside and walked over and sit beside him. Jason put his phone down on the table and looked into my eyes. "Jason, have you found a place yet?" I asked. "No, I haven't." Jason replied. "Have you been looking?" I asked. "I have." Jason said, looking away. His reaction showed me that he hasn't been looking or if he has, he hasn't been looking very hard. I should've never agreed to letting him continue to stay here, when he first asked. I figured it would be good to have him here for the kids but either way it's going to be hard once he decides to leave.

I pulled the papers out the envelope and handed them to Jason. He scanned over the papers and on the last sheet where it said how much I was asking for, I just knew he was going to raise hell about it but he didn't. "Do you have a pen?" Jason asked. "Yes," I said, getting one out the drawer by the stove. I handed the pen to Jason. "Are you okay with the price I'm asking for with the child support and alimony? I think that's fair, especially with your main job and the weekly salary from the church as well. You should be able to live your normal lifestyle plus take care of your financial obligations to our family." I said. "I think It's fair." Jason said.

Jason held the pen in his hand and kept looking over the documents. I just sat there patiently waiting. I don't want him to feel like I'm pressuring him or anything. "Jannice, I know I put you through a lot but please reconsider this divorce. I promise I'll do better. I'll even go to counseling." Jason said, with tears in his eyes. "No Jason. I've gave you chance, after chance, after chance. You disrespected me too many times. Jason I want to ask you something? If I had cheated on you with a man, would you forgive me?" I asked. "No, I probably wouldn't have." Jason said. I know and the sad thing is, I gave you another chance and you did it two more times. And because I thought there was a chance for us and I still didn't want to give up on us or our family, you took my kindness and forgiving spirit for weakness. I can't do this anymore with you." I said.

I felt the tears coming down my face but this time they weren't hurtful tears, they were tears of feeling defeated. As if I wasn't good enough for him that made him keep wanting more from someone else. "Jason, you will never tell me you're going to hang out with your friend Marcus and decided to go hook up with one of your tricks again. I'm letting you be free to be with whoever you choose to be with. You don't have to lie to me ever again. So please sign the papers so we can be free from each other since I could never make you happy before. Maybe you can find someone else to make you happy and so will I." I said.

I got up and went upstairs to get Myra and Jay. "What's up Mom?" Jay asked. "Your father and I need to talk to you both downstairs at the dinner table." I said. "What yall need to talk to us about Mom?" Myra asked. "Well how about you two go downstairs so you can both see." I said. "Okay." Myra said, heading downstairs after Jay.

Jay and Myra both sat at the table, wondering why we're interrupting them from doing what they were doing in their rooms. I sat at the table across from Myra and Jay and I held both their hands. "Look you two, things haven't been going too good with your father and I. We want you both to know that we love you both very much and neither one of you did anything wrong. Sometimes parents just fall out of love with each other and that's what happened between your father and I. Your dad and I are getting a divorce and he'll be moving out soon. You will still see your father on the weekends and after school if you all want to." I said.

Jay stood up from the table. "Daddy, you did this! You cheated on Mom! You did this to our family! You broke our family up! Mom, you can cover up what Dad did all day long, but I know what he's been doing. I've even heard him on the phone a few times, planning to meet these women. Dad, when I grow up and I get married one day, I hope and pray that I'll never be anything like you! You did this and I hate you for it!" Jay, yelled and ran upstairs to his room.

I stood up to follow Jay. "Myra, do you want to come with me to talk to Jay or you want to go back to your room?" I asked. "I'm okay Mommy. I'll let you talk to Jay and I'll just go back to my room." Myra said.

Myra stood up from the table and was about to go upstairs, but she turned around and hugged Jason. "Daddy, I still love you and I love Mommy too." Myra said, as she kissed her father on the cheek. I waited for Myra to go upstairs before I turned to Jason. "Are you happy Jason? Are you happy now? You couldn't stop until you've destroyed this family. Good job! You got exactly what you wanted. Good Job!" I said, heading upstairs.

I knocked on Jay's door and walked in. "Hey handsome. Do you feel like talking?" I asked. "Not really Mom. I just want to listen to some music and then go to bed. Can we talk tomorrow?" Jay asked. "Yes, that's fine. But we definitely need to talk tomorrow." I said. "Okay Mom." Jay replied. "Goodnight baby and don't stay up too late." I said. "I won't Mom." Jay said.

I was about to close the door when Jay called out. "Mom." Jay said. "Yes son," I replied. "I love you and I'm so sorry what Dad did to you." Jay said, getting up from his bed and hugging me tightly. "Thank you baby but you know your mom is a strong black woman right? I just want to make sure you and your sister will be okay." I said. "Mom, we will." Jay said. "I closed Jay's door and went to ask Myra if she wanted to talk but she shook her head no. I'll let them process this and I'll take them out right after school tomorrow.

CHAPTER

11

What you're missing

I just got to work, still a little tired from last night. I didn't sleep much from tossing and turning. I guess I was a little worried about how Jay took the news about us getting a divorce. Myra seemed okay this morning when I helped her get ready for school. While she was getting dressed, Jason knocked on the door and told Myra he was taking today off from work and he was taking her and Jay out today. Jay didn't want to go and didn't want to even see his father's face. I explained to Jay that his father was still his father and no matter how wrong he felt his father's actions were, he still needs to show respect and remember that his father is the adult.

After I talked to Jay and told him to take the day off from school and let his father take them out, he finally agreed to it. Jay smiled and told me he would at least try to be cordial with his father.

I sat down at my desk, waiting for my third graders to enter the classroom. I hope today goes well. I'm not up for any drama today. I gave the class five chapters to read in their reading book and I told them there would be a test afterwards.

I needed some peace and quiet for about thirty minutes or so and what better way to do that then to have them reading. The class seem to have been following my instructions so far. I glanced over the class and saw that Cameron had his hand raised. I motioned for him to come up. "Mrs. Davis, my Uncle Rick told me to give this to you." Cameron said. "Uncle Rick?" I asked with a confused look on my face. "Yes Uncle Rick. He came to talk to you at the PTA meeting. He's dark-skinned, with long dreads." Cameron said, with a look on his face as if I should know who he's talking about. "Ricardo?" I asked. "Yes. I call him Uncle Rick though." Cameron said. "Okay. Well thank you Cameron. Now get back to your desk so you can finish reading. I want you to do well on your test." I said. "Yes ma'am." Cameron said, walking back to his seat.

I opened the letter to see what Mr. Smooth Ricardo is talking about.

"Hey Beautiful,

I just wanted to say hello and see how you're doing. I know you and I have been texting for a few days now and I'm just wondering when can we meet for a drink? I know you're going through a divorce right now and may not be looking for anything serious at the moment, but a friend. Let me be that friend and take you out for a drink. I'm really a nice guy and I promise to be a complete gentleman. Give me a chance."

Talk to you later, Ricardo.

PS. I like to be called Rick though. J"

His letter was quite sweet but who the hell gives a third grader a letter to ask his teacher out. I guess I understand since he knew I would see his nephew since I'm his teacher. I guess I can't be mad at this man's game. Ricardo seems like a nice guy. Maybe I'll have a drink with him tonight. I think it's time for me to show Jason that I'm moving on with my life without him.

I gave the class their test on the few chapters they read. Cameron got a ninety on it. I was so happy to see his progress in his school work. Maybe

Ricardo is helping him with his work and sturdy habits. I gave the class the assignment to finish reading the rest of the story and be ready for another test on tomorrow.

I pulled up to my house and saw Jay outside playing basketball with one of our neighbor's son Twane. "Hey Mom." Jay said, giving me a fist bump, like I'm one of his homeboys. "Boy what is this fist bump thing you're doing?" I asked. "Mom, I'm all sweaty and stuff and you're just getting off from work, looking all beautiful. I don't want to get you dirty." Jay said. "Okay. Good comeback son. I like that response," I replied laughing. Jay burst out laughing as well. "Look, you can stay out here thirty more minutes, then come inside so you can have dinner," I said. "Okay Mom," Jay replied. "Hey Twane. How are you?" I asked. "I'm Okay Mrs. Davis. How are you?" Twane asked. "I'm okay. Would you like to stay for dinner?" I asked. "No ma'am. My mom is making dinner now so I'll eat at my house." Twane said. "Okay. Tell Kathy and your dad I said hello." I replied. "I will." Twane said.

I walked inside and put my things down on the coffee table. I walked in the kitchen and Jason was standing by the stove cooking again. Two days straight of cooking dinner. This is something I can actually get use to but I know that's not happening. As soon as our divorce is final and we sign the paperwork together, he's getting his ass out of here.

I walked next to Jason to see what he's cooking. "Hello. How are you?" I asked. "I'm good Jannice. How are you?" Jason replied. "I'm good, now that I'm home." I said. "Can I have a hug Jannice? You know we don't have to hate each other." Jason said. "You're right," I replied, as I leaned in to give him a hug. I pulled away as soon as he wrapped his arms around me. I don't want him to think he's about to get a quick feel up on me or anything like that.

I sat down at the table. "What's for dinner?" I asked. "I'm making, fried chicken, green beans and yellow rice. We still have the strawberry cheesecake from yesterday that's still in there so we can have that for dessert." Jason said. "Oh that sounds good," I replied.

Jay came inside and was heading upstairs. "Are you going to get in the shower Jay?" I asked. "Yes ma'am I am." Jay said. "Good. Tell your sister to come here please." I said. "Okay Mom," Jay replied.

Myra came downstairs and gave me a big hug. "Hey my little princess. How are you doing?" I asked, giving my baby a kiss on the cheek. "Just dancing in my room. I was reading but I finished that book a little earlier," Myra said. "You love reading don't you baby?" I asked. "I sure do. When I get older, I'm going to write a book Mama," Myra said. "Well, why do you have to be older to do that? You can be a writer right now. All you need is a story-line you want to write about and write your book," I said. "Really Mom? I didn't know I could write a book now at my age," Myra said, sounding excited. "You sure can," I said.

The excitement in my daughter's eyes were priceless. "Mom, I think I'm going to write a book about you and Daddy." Myra said. "About me and your father? And what's that book going to be about?" I asked. "About you and Daddy being in love but one day you both stopped loving each other because you found out Daddy did something he shouldn't have done." Myra said.

My heart just dropped when Myra said that. I looked over in Jason's direction to see his reaction. He was looking as well and then he turned his head, like he was busy cooking. "Bam!" It's amazing what children can hear and see when you think you're hiding something from them and they don't know what's going on. "Well young lady, that sounds like a great book and I can't wait to read it," I replied. "I can't wait for you to read it Mom," Myra said. "Okay. How about you go in the restroom and wash your hands for dinner," I said. "Okay Mommy," Myra said.

I know Jason felt some kind of way when Myra made that comment. I'm glad she did, that way Jason knows his children aren't blind. They see exactly who and what he is. A cheater and a liar. Jason started fixing everyone's food but he didn't look at me or the children. I know what Myra said really hurt him but he brought all this on himself.

Dinner was really good. Jason brought his southern style home cooking out tonight. Jay and Myra must have thought it was great to because they cleaned their plates. I texted Ricardo earlier after I got off from work and asked him if he wanted to have a drink with me tonight. He agreed and I told him I would text him the address after dinner and we could meet at seven-thirty.

I went upstairs and took a shower. I texted Ricardo and told him to meet me at the "Ballroom" and I gave him the address. I've never been there before but Adrienne told me she went there a few times with her cousins. She said it's a nice little casual bar. Adrienne said the crowd is between thirty and fifty. Hell I might even find me a sugar daddy tonight.

I got dressed and did something with my hair. I applied a little make-up and a little lip gloss. After I got dressed I couldn't help from admiring myself in the mirror from head to toe. This red body dress is popping and hitting all my beautiful curves in all the right places. I've been doing my little planks and been working on my abdominal area for the past few months now and a sister stomach is completely flat. Not a bulge or anything. Just the way I like it.

I grabbed my purse and car keys and headed downstairs. The kids were sitting in the den with Jason, watching TV, which is surprisingly since they're normally in their bedrooms. "Hey Mommy. Look at you. You look beautiful. Where you going tonight?" Myra asked. "I'm going out to enjoy myself." I said. "Well you look beautiful Mommy," Myra said. "Thank you sweetheart." I said, giving her a kiss on her forehead. "Mom you do look beautiful. I hope you enjoy yourself and meet someone who will treat you right and treat you the way you deserve to be treated." Jay said.

After Jay made his comment he looked at his father and so did I. I wanted to see Jason's reaction. He ignored Jay's comment and continued looking at the TV. "Jason, I'll see you later on. Have a goodnight kids." I said.

I walked out the door and as I was going to my car, I heard Jason called my name. "Jannice, you're not coming back tonight?" Jason asked, like I just be spending the night away from my children. "Yes. I'll be back tonight," I said. "Where are you going?" Jason asked. "Do you want me to tell you a lie, like what you use to tell me when you were doing your dirt, or should I tell you the truth? Hell, you shouldn't require me to tell you the truth since you don't know anything about the truth right?" I said. "Look Jannice, I know I hurt you but you don't have to do this," Jason said. "Do what?" I asked. "You're going to meet some man," Jason yelled. "Jason, you're a trip," I said, ignoring him as I got in my car.

I drove off watching Jason still standing outside, as if he was expecting me to turn around. It amazed me that he can't take what the hell he dished out. How can you think what you were doing was okay but when I do it,

I'm the worst person in the world? Hell no. If it's good for goose, it's good for the gander.

CHAPTER

12

I'll wait On you

I pulled up to "The Ballroom" and the parking lot was extremely pack for a big Tuesday night. I sure hope it's not this busy inside. I paid the twenty dollars and let the security guard check me. It seems like the man kept touching me more then he should have. "Your good ma'am," the guard said. "Thank you," I replied.

I walked inside and the place was exquisite from top to bottom. I sat at the bar to enjoy the view. If I had to guess, it was probably about eighty people in here. Normally that would be a lot but "The Ballroom" was quite huge. No one was on top of anyone. There was a huge dance floor and a stage set up. I guess that's probably where the bands perform.

I pulled out my phone and texted Ricardo, telling him I was here at the bar. Ricardo responded back saying he was walking inside now. I hope I'm not overdressed or anything. Ricardo and I didn't plan to meet, it was a random thing when I ask if he wanted to meet for a drink. Is this right? How will this look to people if they were to see me out with this man that's not my husband? Well all I'm doing is having a drink or two with Ricardo. It's not like I'm planning on going to bed with him or anything like that.

We're just two people meeting for a drink, which is strictly plutonic. No more, no less and if Jason wasn't a shame to be doing his damn dirt, than why should I feel guilty about having a drink?

Ricardo walked in and he almost took my breath away. He had on a nice black suit, with a white shirt, and a white and black pin stripe bow tie. "Damn he cleans up well. Ricardo spotted me and I smiled and waved at him. He started walking towards me and I swear my heart felt like it missed a few beats. Why am I so nervous? It's not like we're on a date or anything. Ricardo just met me for a few drinks. Just as if he was a colleague or mine. I kept saying it over and over in my head, trying to convince myself that was all to it.

I stood from the bar stool as Ricardo stood in front of me. I quickly extended my hand towards him, stopping him as he was about to lean in to give me a hug. "So a brother can't even get a hug?" Ricardo asked. "Maybe later," I replied. "Okay, I'll take that," Ricardo said, as he pulled out my bar stool for me to sit down. He sat beside me, a little too close for comfort but it was okay I guess.

I could tell that Ricardo was just as nervous as I am. He must not go on too many dates. "Jannice, you look absolutely gorgeous tonight. You got all dressed up for little old me?" Ricardo said, smiling. "Dressed up for you huh?" I replied, laughing. "No, I haven't been out in a long time and I wanted to feel beautiful for a change," I said. "I'm sure you always look beautiful," Ricardo replied. "Well sometimes we just want to feel that way, without waiting for someone to tell us. And you look quite handsome yourself," I said. "Thank you. I try," Ricardo said. "You don't go on many dates do you?" I asked.

Ricardo started laughing, like I just said the funniest thing to him. "Is it that obvious?" Ricardo asked. "Just a little. You just seem a little nervous that's all," I said. "Well, to be honest, most women I meet, only want to smash. They're not looking for anything serious. Well at least not from me," Ricardo said. "Why do you think that is?" I asked, curious to hear his response. "I don't know, maybe that's all they see me as, or maybe they think that's all I want to do. But smashing is cool but sometimes a brother wants more than that too. It would be nice to just chill around the house and watch movies all day, while being cuddled up on the couch with someone special," Ricardo said.

I really wasn't expecting that kind of response from Ricardo but it was nice to hear, even though he might have just been saying that because he wanted to see my reaction from his comment. "So tell me about yourself Mr. Ricardo James?" I asked. "Well, I don't know what you want to hear," Ricardo said. "Just be honest and tell me who you are now, who you use to be and what you want in life?" I asked. "Damn. I never had anyone ask me a question like that while on a date." Ricardo said. "No you mean while having a drink?" I corrected him. "Right, while having a drink." Ricardo said. "Well, I'm not just anyone sir." I said. "I can definitely see that." Ricardo said, smiling.

I must admit that Ricardo had the prettiest smile I've ever seen on a man before. He must have worn braces when he was younger, because his teeth were perfectly straight and white. "Let's get our drinks first and I'll tell you everything about me," Ricardo said.

Ricardo got the bartender's attention. "Hello, can I help you two?" The bartender asked. "Yes, you may. I'll have a rum and coke and the lady will have?" Ricardo said, pointing to me. "I'll have a blue martini," I said. "Sounds good. Coming right up. And by the way, I'm Tiko. In case you guys need anything else." Tiko said. "Thank you Tiko." Ricardo and I both said.

The bar was filling up with a lot more people and a jazz band was playing. The music was really nice and I was definitely enjoying myself and my company as well. "Here you go." Tiko said, as he handed us our drink. "I can put you both on a tab if you would like?" Tiko said. "Okay that sounds good," Ricardo replied. "Okay cool," Tiko said, before fixing another person a drink beside us.

I took a sip of my drink. I haven't had a blue martini in a very long time but it was really good. "So are you going to answer my question about who you are sir?" I asked. "Well, I'm thirty-six years old. I've never been married and I have one son, name LaQuan. He's ten years old and lives in Kannapolis North Carolina, with his mother, step-father and little brother. His mother Tomeka and I were together for about three years until we broke up and she moved on with someone else and two years later, she got married. I get my son every other weekend when I'm not on the road working. I own my own trucking company, with five rigs and four drivers. I see myself owning about six more rigs in the next three to five years' tops.

I hope to find the love of my life and settle down with and have a family. Now tell me about yourself?" Ricardo said.

I took another sip of my drink. "Well I'm thirty five years old and I'm a third grade teacher. I've been a teacher for almost thirteen years. I graduated with my bachelor's in secondary education from Winthrop University and I later earned my master's degree in education as well. I've been married for ten years and I'm currently waiting to finalize my divorce from my husband. We have two children together. I have two very best friends that I've known my entire life. My parents are divorce. My mother is a retired teacher and my father is a retired Warden at a prison. My father remarried about fifteen years ago to someone who is only five years older than me, and they have two daughters, so I have two half-sisters and one brother. Where do I see myself in the future? I plan to be happily divorce, raising my two children and I think I want to go back to school to get my doctorates degree in education," I said. "Wow, that's impressive," Ricardo said.

I just finished my drink. "What's impressive?" I asked. "That you plan to go back to school to get your doctorates, after already having two degrees," Ricardo said. "Well thank you. You know you can never have too much education." I said. "I hear that," Ricardo said. "Did you go to college?" I asked. "Yes I went to community college for two years. I have an associate's degree in business," Ricardo said. "Oh good," I said. "Would you like to dance?" Ricardo asked. "I rather not. I mean, I love to dance but I'm still technically married, so I shouldn't be dancing until I'm a single woman." I said. "Dang, calm down I was only asking for a dance, that's it." Ricardo said. "I understand but my answer still stands. If you would like to get to know me like that then let me get my divorce first. Now if you don't want to wait and you decide to move on, then I can respect that," I said.

Ricardo took my hand into his hand and smiled. "I totally understand Jannice and I would look at you differently if you didn't wait until your divorce was final to deal with me. I know you're not one of these chicken heads out here. You're a classy beautiful woman and I would be a fool to not wait. I've always been told anything worth having is worth fighting for, but in our case, I'll say waiting for. I want you in my life and I'll wait until you're officially divorce, just as long as you're still getting a divorce and not have me just sitting waiting for nothing." Ricardo said. "Trust me, my marriage is over and he knows it. I'm just waiting for the lawyers to say that it's a seal deal," I said. "Good, then I'll wait for you." Ricardo said, as he leaned over and kissed me on my cheek.

CHAPTER

13

I Can Change

I just pulled up in my driveway, after having a few drinks with Ricardo. He seems like a nice guy and I like him. I feel like there's a little more to his story though. Maybe one day he'll feel more comfortable talking to me and sharing more about himself as well. I'm as cut and dry as it gets. I'm a woman who loved her husband and stuck by his side through all his cheating and his dirty deeds. I love my children, my job, my friends, and the rest of my family. That's all to me. I guess I'm as boring and bland as they come.

I walked in the house and put my purse down. I got a bottle of water out the fridge and sat in the den. Jason walked in the den and sat down across from me. He was just staring, not saying a word. "Are you okay?" I asked. "No, I'm not. I want to know how long you're going to do me like this?" Jason asked. "Do you like what Jason? You act like I'm mistreating you. I'm letting you stay here even after you cheated on me, not once, not twice but three times. So tell me how I'm mistreating you?" I asked.

Jason just looked at me and then he shook his head. "I know what I did to you broke you. I did you wrong and made you not be able to trust me. I even hurt our children as well. Jay can't even look at me when he sees me. I say good morning to him and he says "hey" but it's so dry. He doesn't even want to be in my presence. I know I've made a huge mistake but I'm asking you, no I'm begging you to forgive me and give me another chance. I know I don't deserve another chance but Please give me another chance. I'll get counseling and anything else I need to do. Just please don't leave me," Jason said.

I didn't say anything but I heard every single word that came out his mouth. "Jason, first of all you didn't broke me. You might have bruised me a little but you never broke me. But was I just not enough for you? Was our family just not enough for you? Would you be okay if I was the one who was out here cheating? Would you have given me all these chances that I gave you? Could you act like nothing happened and trust me again?" I asked.

I wanted to hear his response. "So was I enough for you?" I asked him again, in case I was speaking too fast for him to comprehend the first time. "Yes you are. I was just being selfish and wanted my cake and eat it to," Jason replied. "What about your children Jason? Were they not enough for you? You've made a complete mess of our lives. Your son can't even look at you like he used to. Shit, I can't look at you like I use to," I said. "Look, would you have been okay if I cheated on you? Do you think you would've forgave me and for once in your life be honest Jason?" I asked.

Jason dropped his head, as if he suddenly couldn't speak or something. "Oh cat has your tongue now? You wanted to talk so let's talk. You stand your ass on the pulpit preaching every Sunday, telling people about sin, and the sins they've committed but what about yours? I wonder how many of your members would stay under your leadership knowing that you're an adulterer and a damn liar. That you constantly cheated on your wife and because I didn't want to break up our family, I stayed with you. After you promised me over and over again that you would stop. Jason, why can't you except the fact that you messed our life up together? We were supposed to grow old together and watch our children grow up. Jason, why couldn't you have honored our wedding vowels we made in front of our family, friends and before God? You're such a hypocrite. I hate I even met you and married you. I thought you would protect me but you're the one I needed protecting from. Jason you tried to break me but you didn't. I'm going to get my life back and live a normal life. And my life doesn't include you in it. Go ahead and live your life with whomever you choose to. You don't have to worry about coming back home to me. You don't even have to think of some half ass excuse to tell me anymore of where you're going or where you've been," I said.

Jason had some confuse look on his face as if he didn't know what I'm talking about. "Jason, if you could do all this over, would you do it differently? Are you sorry you cheated, or sorry you got caught?" I asked. "Jannice, I'm sorry for everything. I really love you from the bottom of my heart. Please come back to me. I don't want to lose you Jannice. Think of our children?" Jason said.

I burst out laughing at what this bastard just said. "Wow, you have the damn audacity to tell me to think of our children? Did you thought of our children when you were heading over to that tramp's house? What about before you stuck your dick inside of her? Did our children cross your mind then? Jason, you're making me hate you right now. I can't go around hating you because I'm a Christian woman but I don't have any love left inside of me for you anymore. So don't try to change for me, you have to want to change for yourself but there's no hope for us anymore. You and I are done and over with. There's no reconciling for us," I said. "So that's it? You're just going to walk away for what we built together?" Jason asked. "Yes. You did," I said, getting off the couch and heading upstairs to shower.

CHAPTER

14

Its your Decision

Today was an okay day. Adrienne and I went to McAllister for lunch. I told Adrienne all about Ricardo and our little drink at "The Ballroom," last night. Of course Adrienne had her concerns about me moving on before my divorce was final. I told her I definitely wasn't jumping into anything until Jason and I sign our divorce papers to end things for good. Adrienne told me she understood that but I still need to be careful. I told her I would.

Sharese and I talked last night before I went to bed and she told me the same thing. Take my time with Ricardo and make sure everything is over with Jason first. Sharese has been in training for a week now in Colorado. Her company is supposed to be getting some new machines in their department so the supervisors has to be trained on how to run them first.

I picked the kids up early from school today so we could visit my mom. It's been about a month now since I've seen her and I'm a shame to say that, especially since she's only forty-five minutes away. Mom is a retired fifth grade teacher and lives in Rock Hill South Carolina. I called her this morning on my way to work to see what she had planned for today. She told me she had a doctor's appointment this morning but would be back home around noon. She asked was I coming over and I told her probably this weekend. I could hear the disappointment in her voice when I said that. I wanted to surprise her with a visit. I've learned a long time ago when you have children, there's always things that can come up so you can't always plan things.

I pulled up in Mom's driveway and texted Jason that I have the kids with me so he won't be worry that something happened. The kids and I got out the car and knocked on the front door. "Oh my God Jannie. I'm going to beat your butt for not telling me you were coming over," Mom said, giving me a kiss on the cheek and hugging me tightly. "I know, I wanted to surprise you Mom," I said, while Mom hugged both the kids. "Look, how big you two have gotten," Mom said, as we walked inside the living room.

I sat down and smelled that delightful aroma that was coming from the kitchen. "Mom, what are you cooking? I asked. "Nothing but Collards, rice, green beans, macaroni and cheese, and bar-be-que ribs." Mom said, with a smile. "Mom, you had a feeling I was coming over didn't you?" I asked. "You know I did." Mom said, as we both laughed. "Mom, you know me too well." I said. "Well I am your one and only mother right?" Mom said, giving me another hug. "That's right. So when is dinner ready?" I asked. "Baby, everything is done now. "You all can get wash up and I'll fix your dinner now." Mom said, as she walked towards the kitchen.

The kids and I washed our hands and went to the kitchen table. Mom had our plates on the table with a big picture of sweet tea in the middle of the table. We held hands, while Mom blessed the food. Everything looks so delicious." Mom, you really out did yourself." I said. "Well, I hope you all enjoy it and I forgot to tell you that the candy yams are in the oven." Mom said. "Sounds good to me," I said.

The kids acted like they were starving. "Mom, have you seen Eugene and Brenda lately?" I asked. "Yes, they came by and ate Sunday dinner with me last Sunday. Those three children of theirs is something else. They aren't well behaved like your children are. I had to keep telling EJ to stop running in the house and he's ten years old. I can tell him that two minutes ago and he turn around and do it again. I told Eugene and Brenda they must not be discipline their children. Of course Brenda look like she had an attitude after I said that but you know I didn't care, "Mom said. "I know you didn't care Mom," I replied.

After dinner the kids went to play on the swing set outside in the backyard. "Mom do you want me to help you with the dishes?" I asked. "Sure thing baby. That would be nice," Mom said. I helped Mom dry the dishes off as she washed them. "Baby why has it took you so long to come see me? That's not like you?" Mom said. "Mom, you just don't know what I've been going through. I just needed to catch my breath and breathe some." I said. Mom looked at me with a strange look as we finished the dishes.

Mom and I sat in the living room. Mom turned the TV down and looked at me, "baby, what's been going on? Are you okay?" Mom, asked. "Mom, things have been crazy in my life. I caught Jason cheating again," I said. "I know Jason isn't doing that mess again?" Mom said. "Yes Mom, he was at it again. I put him out the house that night. He had the nerves to think he was going back home after what I just saw with my own eyes." I said.

Mom just shook her head. "Well baby, how did you catch him?" Mom asked. "I followed him to the woman's house. I waited for a while Mom and how about the woman's husband came back home Mom and caught Jason in his house. Mom, dude beat Jason down like he stole something from him. Jason's face was all bloody and bruised up. The man was stomping, kicking, and all. Now Mom, while that man was beating Jason's behind, I was beating the hell out his wife as well," I said. "I know you didn't," Mom said laughing. "Mom, I was wailing on her. I didn't know if I was fighting her because of her sleeping with my husband or if I was taking everything that Jason ever did out on her. Either way, she wore that behind cutting that night." I said.

Mom shook her head and then burst out laughing again. "You better be careful fighting those chicken heads over Jason. You know people don't fight fair no more." Mom said. "You're so right Mom. But I'm done with Jason behind now Mom. He came back the next night, telling me he had nowhere else to go and can he move back in. I let him move back in but I told him he can only stay until the divorce is final and he had to be home by six o'clock each night." I said. "Why six o'clock?" Mom asked. "So he could be home with the kids and they don't have to be over at the neighbor's house the entire time," I said. "Okay. That makes sense," Mom said.

I know Mom is shocked by me filing for a divorce, just by the expression on her face. "Baby, are you sure you want this divorce?" Mom asked. "Mom, I am. I'm tired of catching him cheating on me and giving him chances after chances after chances. I'm done. I already have the paperwork in and I'm just ready to hear back from my lawyer to let me know when to be at her office to finalize our divorce. I just hope he's looking for a place because, once we sign that line on the divorce papers, he can't come back to my house, other than to get the rest of his things and to get the kids." I said.

Mom just looked at me like she felt sorry for all I had to put up with off Jason. "Mom, I'm not the type of woman that just sits there while her husband is sleeping with any and everything that moves. Jason and I are done and I think he knows that now. Now Mom, he's trying hard to win my back. He's coming home every day by six o'clock and even making breakfast and cooking dinner as well, but once you have done so much to a person, when they walk away and say their done, they really are. Mom I know my worth and I don't mind being alone, especially if I can have a piece of mind with it. It's too much stuff out there to catch, and I'll be damn if I'm going to let Jason bring me something home, that I can't get a shot for." I said.

I almost forgot that I was talking to my mom when I use the word "damn," to her. Maybe she didn't catch that but she knew where that was coming from and angry place that Jason caused me. "Mom, am I doing the right thing?" I asked. "Well baby, if it was me, I probably would've done the same exact thing. You know back in the day, women stayed with their husbands no matter what they were out there doing. If they were cheating, a drunk, on drugs, beating them, they just stayed and took it, because they knew they couldn't make it on their own, especially if they weren't working. Now a days, woman aren't putting up with any of that mess now, because most woman are making money, and making good money that they don't have to put up with any nonsense. But I think I would've done the same thing you're doing. It's too much stuff out there to catch, dealing with a cheating husband. But baby, I can't make that decision for you. This is your decision and yours alone." Mom said. "You're right Mom and I love you for your opinion." I replied.

We had a delightful evening with Mom and the kids enjoyed themselves as well. Mom sent plates back. She even sent one back for Jason, even though I told her she didn't have to send him one. Jason was eating all before, so I'm sure he's already ate dinner by now. As I was driving home, I thought about what Mom said to me, that she would've done the same thing, but this was my decision to make. I think deep down, I'm making the right decision to be free from Jason and ready to have a new start on life.

CHAPTER

15

Wine & Dine

I just got off from work and Sharese sent Adrienne and I a text saying "Wine and Dine" at her house at six o'clock. I'm a little tired from my drive yesterday and staying up later than normal watching TV, but I can't pass up the opportunity to see my girls. I texted back telling her to count me in. I went over to the grocery store and grabbed a bottle of wine and a lemon pound cake for dessert. The last time we didn't have anything sweet to eat and I definitely wanted something.

I pulled up at Sharese house at six-o'clock on the dot. Adrienne Lexus was in the driveway already. I knocked on the door, waiting for Sharese to come to the door. "Hey girl. How are you?" Sharese said, as she gave me a hug. "It's good to see you. This week of training kicked my ass." Sharese said. "I'm sure it did. Is it beautiful up there?" I asked, always wanting to go to Colorado. "It is. Nice, clean, crisp air. Beautiful Mountains and freaking bears all over the damn place. You see bears up there like you see deers down here in the dirty south." Sharese said. "Oh wow. I'm glad to see you made it back safely." I said. "I know but everything is okay with you right?" Sharese asked. "Well that's why it's our wine & dine, right?" I said. "That's right." Adrienne chimed in, as she gave me a hug.

We sat down and dived in. "Girls, Mom told me to tell you both hello." I said. "Oh Lord. How is Aunt Jackie doing? I totally forgot you went there yesterday." Adrienne said. "Mom is doing well. She looked good to. She told me she is still doing her aerobics exercise each morning." I said. "Well, that's good. "Please tell her we said hello." Adrienne said. "I certainly will. I told her about me filing for divorce." I said. "Oh Lord, and what did she say?" Sharese asked. "She understood and told me if it was her, she probably would do the same thing as well. Mama dealt with my father's affairs for years until one day she just got tired of it and told him to get out. My brother and I always knew what Daddy was out there doing and my mother did as well. I remember my brother saw Daddy with another woman and he told my mother about it and she whipped him and told him to stay out of grown people's business. I later waited a few hours after she cooled down from whipping my brother and I told her, that you can't beat us all day for you being upset with what Daddy's out there doing, but we're not out there cheating on her. Her frustration and anger should be taken out on my Daddy and not on us because we're not stupid and we know what he's out there doing." I said.

Adrienne and Sharese mouth dropped as if I told my mother this today. "Girl, you never told us you told your mom that. Because we know Aunt Jackie do not play. I bet Aunt Jackie whipped your ass when you said that, huh?" Sharese asked. "No, she just looked at me like she was about to though, so after I said what I said, I haul ass in my bedroom and got up under the bed, because I know I was about to get a whipping as well. But she never did, instead she went to my brother's room and apologized to him for her taking her anger out on him about something she knew for a long time. Mama was just mad that now we knew his dark secret and she hated him even more for it. That night when he came home at ten o'clock, after getting off work at four. She told him to get out. Mama told him to go lay back up with the whore he was laying with all day. See, that's why I'm getting this divorce because I refuse to endure what my mother took off my dad. I don't want Myra growing up thinking that's how a man is supposed to treat a woman, because she watched how her father treated me, and how allowed him to treat me. And I definitely don't want Jay thinking that men are supposed to treat their girlfriends and wives like that." I said.

I poured myself another glass of wine and took a deep breath. "You know, I wonder why parents do certain things around their children and they wonder why their children turn out to be the way they are? Do you all remember Walena Baxter from high school?" I asked. "I think. Wasn't she that fast ass girl that slept with everyone's boyfriend and husband? That damn girl didn't care who the man was, how old he was, whether he had a girlfriend or a wife or anything. All she wanted was to screw." Sharese said. "Well my Daddy use to mess with her mom. I remember my brother and I was walking home one night from the game and we walked by their house. My brother and I heard loud moaning outside by her house. Now you all know how nosey kids are so my brother and I sneaked in the yard and peeked around the house. Walena's mom Frankie was in the backyard bend over a picnic table screwing two men at the same time.

My brother and I couldn't believe what she was out there doing in the backyard, with no damn shame in the world. As we were running out the yard, we saw Walena sitting on the front porch. She said "did yall enjoy the show?" I looked at her and told her that her mom is a whore. She told me now you know why she's the way she is," I said. "Why didn't you tell us this?" Adrienne asked. "Adrienne, that isn't something you go around telling people about someone's mother." I said. "Whatever happened to Walena?" Sharese asked. "She got hooked on drugs and started prostituting. They found her body by the dumpsters five years ago. She had six children that she left behind. Parents has to be careful what they're doing around their children and what they're allowing them to see. I can't smoke weed and crack every night in the carport but tell my children not to do it. A lot of children do what they see." I said. "That's right." Adrienne and Sharese said.

` This was my second glass of wine and a sister was feeling good. "Sharese, how was your training?" I asked. "It was nice. I wish it was more pleasure than business but it was good. "Sharese said. "How many of you all went?" I asked. "Four of us. Me, Donna, Levar, and Scott." Sharese said. "Okay, who is Scott? Now I've heard you mention Donna, Levar, Shelly, and Ross before but never a Scott, before." I said. Sharese started smiling when she started talking about Scott. Then she had a glow all of a sudden.

"Well, Scott is a new engineer and he's only been with the company for about four months now. This is our first training together. Scott is about six feet tall, one hundred and ninety pounds and has a bald head. His sideburns connect to his beard and goatee. He's extremely handsome and has a muscular tone body.

Scott asked me out a few times before but I didn't want to get involved with anyone at work. He asked me to have dinner with him a week ago before we went out of town for training. I knew I was hungry and needed to eat so I accepted his dinner invitation. Scott made me laugh the entire night while we drank wine and enjoyed our dinner. So that one night turned into about three nights and during training we went out about three more times. So we had like six or seven dates so far. I think I like him and I'm excited to see where this is going to lead us if it leads us anywhere." Sharese said.

It's been a long time since I saw my friend smiled with excitement, since her last breakup with Bradford. "I do need to tell you both that Scott is white." Sharese said. "No shit Sherlock. I think we both kind of figured that out." I said, as Adrienne nodded her head as well. "How do you two feel about that?" Sharese asked. "Girl, this is your life. As long as you're happy, we're happy." I said. "Thank you Jannie." Sharese said. "You're welcome." I said.

I turned and looked at Adrienne. "What's new going on in your life? Any new love interest?" I asked. "No love interest at all. It's just me, Jermaine, my job, and my two best friends. That's it. I do have something new coming up this week but I'll know for sure Monday. I don't want to jinx's anything by telling you both so when it's official then I'll share it with you both." Adrienne said. "Okay. Who knows, maybe Mr. Scott may have some single friends that's looking to meet a beautiful, chocolate, intelligent, well-established sister. You might need to try something new in your life." I said. "I'm won't turn that idea down but I think I'll let him find me. I'm not about to go out there looking for no one." Adrienne said. "Okay. I hear that." I said.

We finished eating and drinking the rest of the wine. We sat around the house still talking and trying to sober up some before we head back home. I told Sharese and Adrienne a little more about that night that

Ricardo and I hung out at "The Ballroom." They had plenty of questions, which I tried to answer all their question, but Lord they sure had a lot.

They seemed okay with it but they still told me to be careful with seeing someone until my divorce is final, otherwise Jason could try to use that against me. I told them I will do just that because knowing his nasty ass, he just might try that.

CHAPTER

16

Sign The Papers

Today is the day that I'm going to be a free woman. Rae called me last night and told me that she had some good news for me. She told me that I can come in at ten o'clock in the morning, a long with Jason and we could sign the divorce papers. I was over joy that I couldn't help the scream that I yelled out into the phone. I apologized for screaming in Rae's ear. Rae laughed and told me it definitely wasn't a problem, since she knew what I was going through. I asked her if she needed me to tell Jason about us meeting in the morning but she said she would do that.

I explained to Rae that Jason was staying in the guest room to be near the kids until our divorce was final. Rae paused for a few seconds and then told me that was a little unusual for her, because most women wanted their husbands totally out the house after they caught them with someone else. I agreed and told her having him here was saving me money to be paying someone to watch them until I got off work.

I told Adrienne last night that I would have to take off today to finalize my divorce. Adrienne told me to handle my business and to call her later when everything was over with. I pulled up to Rae's office and saw that Jason was already here. I recognized Rae's black Denali but not the maroon Jaguar beside Jason's car. It's probably Jason's lawyer's car.

I opened the door and walked inside. "Hey Mrs. Davis. Ms. Spencer is waiting for you in the conference room." The receptionist said. "Okay. Should I go on back?" I asked. "Yes, go ahead." The receptionist said.

I walked back and knocked on the door. "Come in," Rae said. I walked inside with a cheerful look on my face and in a great mood. "Hello," I said. "Hey there Jannice." Rae said, as she extended her hand to me. "So good to see you again Ms. Spencer." I said, as I sat down beside Rae. Rae looked inside her folder and gave Jason's lawyer a copy of the divorce papers.

Jason's lawyer wasn't pretty at all. At first I thought he could possibly be sleeping with her but I'm sure he's not. His lawyer actually looks like a little cartoon character of some sort and with a Mohawk haircut. She flashed a little fake smile at me but I smiled back. "Hey Jason." I said. "Hey Jannice. You look nice this morning." Jason said. "Thank you. So do you." I replied.

Jason's lawyer looked over the documents and slid it back on the table. "Five thousand dollars. That's all Mr. Davis is willing to pay." The lawyer said. "What! Five thousand dollars! That will barely cover the mortgage and the house utility bills." I said. "Well, I guess you're going to have to make that work!" The lawyer said. "Hell no! That won't work!" Rae said.

I slammed the papers in front of Jason. "Is that what you want?" I asked. Jason looked away from me. "Yes It is," Jason said, not looking me in the eyes. "Now you do know I'm entitled to everything down the middle and the house right? I could take half of everything in the bank but I'm not going to do that but you need to give me what I'm asking for." I said. "I think I'll do what my lawyer suggest." Jason said. "Jason, and Judith, I think my client and I will see you in court." Rae said. "How are you going to do that with no proof? All you have is your witness little woman intuition that her husband has been cheating on her and that's it." Jason's ugly ass lawyer said. "Who doesn't have proof? I have proof." I said. "Oh you do. What proof do you have?" Judith asked. "Yes, I do but I need five minutes with my husband." I said. "Jannice, I don't recommend this. We can go to court and get a lot more." Rae said. "And how long will that take?" I asked. "Maybe about three to six months but I'm sure the judge will see it our way." Rae said. "Hell no that's too long. Rae can I have five minutes with Jason please. That's all I need." I said.

Rae stood up from the table with a worried look on her face. "Rae, I'll be fine. Just five minutes is all I need." I said. "Okay, we'll be right outside the door." Rae said. "Thank you." I said.

Jason's lawyer and Rae walked out the conference room to give us some privacy. "Jason, what is the meaning for all this? This wasn't what you and I agreed on when you signed the papers. You even told me that it was fine when I asked you about it. So what the hell are you doing?" I asked. "I'm just not ready to let this go Jannice. I love you and my family." Jason said. "Look Jason, I have the video of you at this woman's house and when the man beat your ass in his front yard. I have that on my phone and Jason I know all about Tyler. You do remember Tyler right, your son?" I said.

Jason's eyes grew wide as hell. "You know about Tyler?" Jason asked. "Yes I do. I been knew about your six year old son. Look what you did to our family and you think I'm going to endure this any longer? The best thing you can do is give me what I'm asking for and give me my divorce, because if you try to prolong this and fight me on this, all your dirty laundry will be exposed and trust me by the time I get up on that pulpit and tell my story, not a church around here would even want you to drive by their church. I think the church will love to know what I've put up with off my husband in all the ten years we've been married. Please don't think I won't destroy you. Jason do the right thing," I said.

Jason had the look of defeat on his face that he knew he had lost and not a leg to stand on. "Jason signed the papers so we can move on. You can have your life back and I can live mine. Maybe one day we can be friends eventually if you want but as of now I want my divorce." I said. "I'll sign the papers and I'll be out the house today. Jannice, I know I messed up and I wish you would give me another chance but I know you won't, but just know I love you. And please except my apology." Jason said. "I except your apology Jason, now it's time for us to move on so we can heal." I said.

I got up and walked around the table and opened my arms. Jason excepted my embrace and he held me for what seemed like forever. "I'm so sorry Jannice. I'm so sorry." Jason said, as he wept in my arms as if he was a little child saying goodbye to his mother. "It's okay Jason." I said, as I kissed him on the cheek. I think Jason realized it was time to let it go and say our final goodbyes as a married couple.

CHAPTER

17

A Free Woman

I walked out Ms. Desiree Spencer's office as a free divorce woman. I will always love Jason because of our children and the life we've built together. I hope Jason finds his happiness and can be happy with the next person that walks in his life, instead of being with multiple women. I just hope he values them and not step all over them the way he did me.

I called Adrienne and Sharese up on three-way. "Hey you two. Guess what? I'm a single free woman and ready to celebrate," I said. "Congratulations free woman." Sharese said, laughing. "Thank you. Look, let's all go out tonight to "The Ballroom," I said. "The Ballroom? Isn't that the place you went the other night with your friend Ricardo?" Adrienne asked. "Yes it is. Are you both available tonight around seven?" I asked. "Yes I am." Sharese said. "I should be able to. I'll see if Deidra can watch Jermaine tonight and I'll definitely be there." Adrienne said. "Sounds good. I'll see you both there at seven o'clock." I said. "Okay, we'll be there." Sharese and Adrienne said. "Good. I'll talk to you both later." I said, hanging up the phone.

I hung up the phone off three-way and called Sharese back. "Hey Jannie. What are you up to, because I know that's why you're calling me back." Sharese said, laughing. "Damn, I swear you know me like a freaking book," I said, slightly annoyed. "Shit, I should. I'm only five minutes older than you." Sharese said, laughing. "Look, let's make it a couples thing. You invite Scott and I'll invite Ricardo," I said. "Oh no you're playing matchmaker and you're not about to get me involved in this for Adrienne to kill us both." Sharese said. "Let me handle that part. I know a handsome guy that likes Adrienne but he was kind of nervous to ask her out. Now let's just say he doesn't have to ask her out, I'll be the one inviting him out to talk to her." I said. "Shit Jannie. I hope this doesn't backfire in our face. Well your face since you're the one setting this up." Sharese said. "Well damn, I guess I can tell you'll be ready to throw me under the bus I see." I said. "Damn right. Adrienne aint killing me." Sharese said. "Okay, just tell me that you'll bring Scott and I'll take care of everything else," I said. "Okay. I'll bring him." Sharese said. "Good. Talk to you later and Sharese dress classy, like red carpet style." I said. "Oh shit you doing this shit big, I see." Sharese said. "Damn right." I replied.

I called Ricardo to see what he was doing tonight. "Hey beautiful. How are you?" Ricardo asked. "I'm okay. Guess what?" I asked. "What's that?" Ricardo asked. "My divorce is final. I'm now a free woman." I said. "Wow! I'm happy for you. We should celebrate." Ricardo said. "I'm going to "The Ballroom," tonight and my two best friends are coming as well. Would you like to be my date?" I asked. "I would love to." Ricardo said. "Good, meet me there at seven." I said. "Okay, sounds good." Ricardo said. "Okay, I'll see you tonight," I said hanging up the phone.

I decided to call Nicolas up and invite him to my little event. I don't know much about Nicolas other than he was divorce and around our age and extremely handsome. Nicolas is the principal of the Junior High School, two blocks down from our school. We met him at a Christmas party two years ago and he seem to like Adrienne, judging by the way he was blushing around her. I wonder if he would like to join us tonight.

I got Nicolas cell number from the receptionist there, Anna. Anna and I went to school together and she told me she could lose her job if Nicolas find out. I told her I would never tell she gave me his number. I hesitated about calling him but I knew they would hit it off well. Adrienne is going to talk shit to me for meddling in her business but I was willing to take that chance for her happiness. I quickly called Nicolas and explained to him what was going on and told him to please join us for the event. He was actually happy I called him and said he was looking forward to tonight. I told him the attire and told him to put on his red carpet outfit. He laughed and told me he would do his best.

I walked in the house and saw all Jason's things packed up and sitting in the dining room. Just seeing Jason things made me realize that our marriage is really over with. This was a man I loved for over ten years, since I met him after college and now it's over.

I walked upstairs and saw Jason coming out the restroom. "Hey Jannice. How are you?" Jason asked. "I'm good. How are you?" I asked. "I'm okay. Look I know I'm supposed to be out the house today but do you mind if I leave Saturday? I just need to tie up some lose ends with my apartment." Jason said. "I'm okay with that. You can stay until Sunday if you would like. So you found an apartment?" I asked. "Yes I did. It's not far from the children's school, so I can pick them up and spend more time with them." Jason said. "Well, I'm glad to hear that. The kids are next door and they know to come back in the next hour so they can eat dinner. I can cook dinner before I leave out, if you want." I said.

Jason walked up closer to me. "You're going out tonight?" Jason asked. "Yes, Adrienne and Sharese are taking me out." I said. "Why? Oh to celebrate your divorce from me huh?" Jason said. I wanted to tell him hell yeah but I didn't say anything. "Jannice, I know you may hate me right now but I'll always love you. "Jason said. "Jason, I don't hate you at all, but sometimes you can be looking for something you don't have and lose everything that you do have. I guess you see the grass isn't greener on the other side," I said.

I went in the kitchen and started making dinner. I know I don't have a lot of time before I have to get ready for tonight. I made the quickest and easiest meal I could put together, which is spaghetti. The kids love spaghetti so they will enjoy their dinner.

I finished making dinner and went upstairs to jump in the shower. I took out my royal blue dress and put it on and did something to my hair. I looked in the mirror and I finally saw the new single woman that I deserve to be. I grabbed my keys off the table and headed out the door.

I arrived at "The Ballroom," and spotted Adrienne standing by the door in a black dress. She looked beautiful and a little lost. "Hey girl." I said, giving her a hug. "Hey Jannice. You see I made it." Adrienne said. "You look absolutely beautiful." I said. "You look beautiful as well." Adrienne said. "Thank you." I replied.

We walked inside "The Ballroom," and Sharese and this handsome white guy was sitting at a table. Adrienne and I walked up to their table. "Hey you two." I said. "Hey there." Sharese said, getting up to hug both Adrienne and I. "Scott, these are my two best friends. "This is Jannice, the lady of the hour and my other best friend Adrienne. Ladies this is my handsome boyfriend, Scott." Sharese said. "So nice to meet you both." Scott said, as he hugged us both." Please join us." Scott said, as he slid two chairs out for both Adrienne and I to sit.

I looked at my phone and saw that Ricardo texted me that he was walking up now. Ricardo walked in, wearing a black suit and a royal blue shirt, the same exact color of my blue dress. His dreads sparkled in the light and that blue displayed his beautiful dark chocolate skin, perfectly.

Ricardo walked over to our table and greeted me with a kiss on my cheek and a hug. "Hey there beautiful." Ricardo said. "Hey there handsome." I said, with a smile. "Ricardo, I want you to meet my two best friends. Sharese and Adrienne and this handsome gentleman is Sharese's boyfriend Scott. Ladies and Scott, this is my friend Ricardo." I said. Ricardo hugged both Adrienne and Sharese and then hugged Scott as well. Scott smiled. "I'm sorry Scott but I'm a hugger so I hope you're okay with that. I'm not trying to come on to you or anything." Ricardo said, laughing. Scott burst out laughing and so did Sharese and I.

Adrienne had her face all boxed up and I could tell she was already pissed with us. Adrienne got up and rolled her eyes. "Excuse me for a second," Adrienne said. I know what that look was about. "Ricardo and Scott, we'll be right back." I said, as Sharese and I got up immediately to follow Adrienne.

Adrienne looked angry as if she was ready to take our heads off. "Adrienne, are you okay?" I asked. "Hell no. How dare you two had me come here, knowing I would be here by myself, without a date. That's just fucking Evil!" Adrienne yelled. "How about you calm your ass down, you're causing a scene." I said. "I don't care." Adrienne said, going the hell off and pointing her finer at us, as if we were ten years old again. I didn't say anything when I saw Nicolas walked up behind Adrienne.

Nicolas tapped Adrienne on the shoulder, as she turned around. "Hello, Adrienne. How are you?" Nicolas said, as he reached in to give her a hug. "Oh my God Nicolas. What are you doing here?" Adrienne asked. "I was invited to celebrate with Jannice and she asked If I would come and maybe I would get the opportunity to talk and dance with you." Nicolas said, smiling. Nicolas turned to shake Sharese and my hand. "You two look nice." Nicolas said. "Thank you Nicolas and so do you." I said. "You two. I swear. I was about to let your ass have it." Adrienne said, laughing and pointing at us. "I didn't have one thing to do with it Adrienne. It was all Jannie." Sharese said, throwing me under the bus.

We all walked back over to the table, where Ricardo and Scott were sitting. "I thought you ladies got lost." Scott said, smiling. "No we didn't. We were just waiting on Nicolas to join us." I said. "Nicolas, this is my friend Ricardo and this is Scott, Sharese's boyfriend. Ricardo and Scott, this is a friend of mine and Adrienne, Nicolas." I said, introducing them.

We all sat down and were enjoying conversation when the waiter came to the table. I order two bottles of wine. We all poured ourselves a glass. "I want to make a toast please." I said, as everyone raised their glasses in the air. "Well today is the day I become a free woman. Meaning my divorce is final. I'm looking forward to living my best life in no regret." I said. Everyone toasted their glass. "Cheers to you free woman." Adrienne said. "Thank you all." I said.

CHAPTER

18

A New Position

After my little gathering last night, Adrienne told me to come to her office this morning. I asked for what but she told me to just be at her office before I go to my class. I knocked on Adrienne's office door and she told me to come on in.

I opened her door and sat in the chair across from her desk. "What's up Adrienne?" I asked. "Good morning to you. Girl, I had a fantastic time last night. Everything was so nice with the music and the drinks and all. They were all very impressed." Adrienne said.

Adrienne seem to be in a great mood, so I know she's not going to fire me. "How did things go with you and Nicolas?" I asked. "It was really nice. Nicolas followed me home and we sat on the front porch and talked for about two hours." Adrienne said. "That's great. Are you going to see him again?" I asked. "Yes, we're going out tonight to dinner and I'm looking forward to it." Adrienne said. "I'm so happy to hear that." I replied.

Adrienne sat straight up in her chair, with a serious look on her face. "Jannie, I called you in here to discuss a serious matter. As you know I have my Doctorate's in education, so I've been applying for a few jobs over the past few months. So last week I heard back from two districts. I've been offered a job as their new superintendent over District two. The reason I called you in here is because they're going to have to find a new principal to replace me here. I want you to be the principal here. You're more than qualified and I think you can definitely do it. Are you interested? Adrienne asked.

My mouth dropped when Adrienne offered me the principal position. I always wanted to step up to the plate and I knew this would be my opportunity to do so. If I don't jump at this opportunity, I may not get another one. I'm going to miss teaching but I need this promotion. "Yes Adrienne. I want it." I said. "Jannie, that's fantastic. No one else would do a better job than you would, plus you've been here at this school for thirteen years right?" Adrienne asked. "Yes, it's coming up on my thirteenth year." I said, proudly. "You deserve it and I'm glad you're not going to let this opportunity pass you by." Adrienne said.

I stood and was about to walk out the door before I realize, I didn't asked Adrienne how much of a pay increase will I get. "Adrienne, how much more will I get for being a principal?" I asked. "I was wondering when you were going to ask me that question. You'll go to eighty-five thousand and after two years, they revaluate you and you can possibly get five thousand on top of your salary. I know the principal position won't make you rich but you'll be able to live a nice comfortable life." Adrienne said. "Okay, that sounds good. Let me get back to my class and thank you for considering me. I'll gladly accept." I said. "Good, we can go over the paperwork by the end of the week and you'll be ready." Adrienne said.

I headed down to my classroom, still can't believe that I got promoted from a teacher to now a principal. I wonder if I would've been considered if Adrienne wasn't my best friend? I wouldn't be surprise if some of these hating teachers start looking for another job after they find out that I'm going to be the new principal. I know I would like to see about five teachers that I want to see gone. Some people lack the sincerity to even be a teacher and these five teachers definitely do.

CHAPTER

19

Too Late for Us

Ricardo texted me around lunch time and asked could he take me out for dinner tonight. I told him I was free tonight and I would like to. He told me to meet him at Ruth Chris at seven o'clock tonight. I told him, I'll see him then.

I'm a little excited because technically this is our first real date. The first time he just met me at the Ballroom for a drink and last night was my "free woman celebration," outing so that didn't count as a date but this will be the first date for us.

I just got off work so excited about my promotion and my date tonight. Jason and I have been doing good as far as us living together under the same roof, while still being there for our children. I basically have somewhere to go every night and he's here with the kids. Which I don't feel bad about doing since he's been doing it forever. Out with his little whores while I was in the house with the children, so I guess he's just getting a little dose of what I was doing.

I sat down on the couch in the den and turned the TV on. The house was quiet. The kids must be in their bedrooms doing their homework.

Jason walked out the guest room into the kitchen. "Hey Jannice. How are you?" Jason asked. "Hey there and I'm fine. How about you?" I asked. "I'm good. Do you have time to talk?" Jason asked. "I do," I replied, wondering what Jason wanted to talk about.

Jason came in the den and sat across from me. "Look, I know you probably don't want to come back to our church anymore but don't you think you should at least come and tell our members that we're divorce and that you're leaving the church? I mean, that way if you were to happen to run into one of our church members or their kids somewhere, they won't think you're just out there running wild or something?" Jason said.

I looked at Jason with a serious look on my face and then burst out laughing. "Are you serious right now? Jason, running wild or something? Really? Or do you mean out there like you were?" I asked. "Well if you want to call it that?" Jason replied. "Hell, I call it like it is. But you do have a small point though. These people look up to me and respected me. So I think I do owe them an explanation. But what do I tell them Jason? That I'm no longer their first lady because my husband couldn't keep his vowels to me and was screwing everything that moves or do I just make up a lie, like all the lies you've told them through the years?" I asked. "You don't have to go into details. Just tell them that we're divorce and have moved on with our lives." Jason said. "No! If you want me to tell them that we're divorce, I'm going to tell them exactly why." I said.

Jason stood up from the couch and just stared at me. "Jannice, are we ever going to get pass this and you forgive me?" Jason asked. "Jason, I have forgiven you. I pray every night to ask God to please remove the hate from my heart that I have for you. I told God that love is way stronger than hate. Even though I have forgiven you, doesn't mean I have forgot it. So God has taken the hate from me but the pain and hurt is still there, but you're not worth anymore of my tears. But if you want me to give the church my final farewell, I will but don't tell me what to say. It's no telling what I will say when I'm up there," I said. "Just do whatever you feel." Jason said.

I got up and took my shower to get away from Jason stupid ass. He wants me to tell the church about our divorce but he wants to dictate what I say and that's not happening. Not now, not ever.

I looked at myself one last time in the mirror and then grabbed my car keys off the dresser. I walked downstairs and Jason was coming out of the guestroom. He looked me up and down and then turned his head. I know his questions was about to come up and I was going to answer what I decide to answer. "Are you going out again tonight?" Jason asked. I ignored his comment and went to the kid's room to kiss them before I left. "Jannice, I still love you and I'll never stop loving you." Jason said. I closed the front door behind me and shook my head. It's a little too late for your undying love now. I just wish our love back then could've kept you from cheating but it didn't.

CHAPTER

20

Laying it on the Table

I was running a little late for dinner with Ricardo. I'm supposed to meet him at seven o'clock but it's seven-fifteen. I hate being late for anything, especially if it's out of my control. I texted Ricardo and told him I was caught in traffic and would be there in three minutes. He sent a smiley face and told me to take my time and he wasn't going anywhere.

I smiled when I read his response. Is it possible that Ricardo is the one for me? I don't know how that would work, a formal first lady and now I'm dating a thug. I pulled up at the restaurant and walked inside. The restaurant wasn't packed at all, which is a surprise. I called Ricardo and told him I was upfront.

Ricardo came upfront and greeted me with a friendly hug. "Hey there beautiful lady." Ricardo said. "Hey to you." I said, as he released me from our embrace. "Our table is this way," Ricardo said. I followed him to our table. "I got us a bottle of wine. I hope that's okay." Ricardo replied.

Ricardo pulled my chair out as I sat down. He looked so nice in his red Ralph Lauren Polo collared shirt and blue slacks. I can tell that Ricardo took pleasure in dressing and looking nice, which I like. "You look very handsome in your red Polo shirt." I said. "Thank you Jannice. You know I have a lot of nice clothes that I never wear." Ricardo said. "And why is that?" I asked. "Because I never go anywhere and it wasn't like I was going on dates or anything anyway." Ricardo said. "Why is that?" I asked, curious at his response." I guess I just haven't met the right lady, until now." Ricardo said, as he touched my hand and smiled.

I returned his smile because I really think that Ricardo wants a good woman in his life. "So you think I could be the one?" I asked. "I mean from what I'm seeing, you definitely could be. Could you see yourself dating me? I'm sure I'm not the kind of guy that you've dated before." Ricardo said. "To be honest, you're not, but Ricardo I heard a saying before, "if you keep doing the same thing you've done before, then you may continue getting the same results that you've always had," or something like that." I said laughing. Ricardo laughed out as well. "But I'm looking for a new beginning with someone new and much different than what I had before." I said.

Ricardo squeezed my hand and smiled. "I like that" Ricardo said. It's something so genuine about Ricardo that I love but I just have the strangest feeling that there's something big that he wants to tell me but he's afraid of my reaction to it.

The server took our order and we just sat in silence for what seemed like over five minutes. It was obvious Ricardo didn't know what to say and to be honest neither did I. I think our nerves was taking more over our date then we had control of, which is crazy since this is our third time hanging out together. Maybe the fact of us labeling as "our first real date" made it a little more exciting and awkward at the same time.

Ricardo poured us a glass of wine, which was fine because it would definitely help me loosen up a little and Ricardo must have felt the same way as well. "Ricardo tell me a secret about you, that some people may not know about you?" I asked, hoping that would break the ice a little.

I was waiting for Ricardo to start talking when he suddenly grabbed my hand and squeeze it. "Okay I will, but Jannice please don't judge me." Ricardo said, with a serious look on his face. It was something in his eyes that did something to me, as if what he was about to tell me was weighting on him deeply. "Jannice, I was locked up for drugs for ten years." Ricardo said.

Before I knew it, I pulled my hand away, without even thinking. "Locked up for drugs?" I asked, wanting to make sure I heard him correctly. "Yes, that's correct. You see Jannice, I was a big time drug dealer when I was younger. I made plenty and I do mean plenty of money. I put all my money in an offshore account and it collected a lot of interest on my money. The police confiscated everything that was in my name, other than my account since it was technically in my mother's name," Ricardo said.

I closed my eyes just to make sure that I was actually hearing Ricardo correctly. "Jannice, I know this is a lot to handle but if it's too much for you and you don't want us to get to know each other any further, I'll totally understand," Ricardo said. "Ricardo, why are you telling me this?" I asked. "Jannice, I've been told growing up, "if you keep hiding something from people you care about, it will eventually come out and you could possibly lose that person with what you should've told them from the start." I'm not proud of what I did at all but I was young. Once I got out of prison, I took my money and I started my own trucking business. I'm doing extremely well because I have four truck drivers that work for me." Ricardo said.

I heard what Ricardo was telling me and I respected him for telling me the truth about himself but is this something I really want to deal with? "Ricardo, are you still involve in that lifestyle, because if you are then I can't be involved in that." I have two children that are my world and I can't have them around any negativity. I was a first lady for eight years of my life and to now be involved with someone who's into drugs, will not work for me at all." I said.

Ricardo touched my face. "Jannice, that's not who I am anymore. That part of my life is over with. I'm on the straight and narrow and I know what I want. I want a life with you, if you think you can look past my past and let's start a new life together." Ricardo said.

I heard every word that was coming out of Ricardo's mouth but is this a road I want to take? Can I be the one that can keep this man away from going back to that kind of lifestyle or drugs and crime? There's no telling how many lives he's destroyed or ruined by the drugs he sold to all these people, but I've made some bad mistakes in my life as well, like loving a man for all these years, knowing what he was out there doing and I still stayed by him. I've dealt with these chicks calling my house in the wee hours of the morning and when I would answer the phone, they would hang the phone up.

I don't want to walk away from Ricardo because of his past and he's actually a changed man. If so, I would be judging him, instead of letting God judge him. "Ricardo, I'm not going anywhere, just as long as you're done with that kind of lifestyle and you're honest with me," I said. "I am." Ricardo said.

I knew since Ricardo was laying everything on the table, it was time for me to tell him about Jason and the fact he was still living with me. "Ricardo, my ex-husband Jason is still living with me." I said. "What? I thought you two just got a divorce?" Ricardo asked. "We are divorce. You see when I put him out, he came by the next few days saying he didn't have any place to go. So I allowed him to come stay in the guestroom in my house. He's been there for the kids and making them dinner and all, things he should've been doing anyway." I said. "So is it over between you two for good?" Ricardo asked. "Yes it's been over with, ever since I caught him over at his little side chick's house." I said. "Good so we have everything out on the table now with no secrets?" Ricardo asked. "Yes, we do." I said. "No secrets," I said. "Well it's good to know that," Ricardo said. "I agree," I replied.

CHAPTER

21

Farewell Red Hill

Ricardo and I have been going out pretty heavy now and things have been going pretty good between us. I sat up in bed and decided to go to church this morning. I felt like I did owe the church an explanation of why I'm not longer attending the church. I'm sure the members are curious to know why I haven't been there. It's been about a month and a half now since I stepped inside Red Hill. I can't just leave them hanging, especially since there's a few members that I'm quite fond of.

I got up and showered and put on a black and white dress. As soon as I say my final farewell to the church, I'm leaving. Jason was right when he said, that I could possibly run up into some of the church members and I'm with someone, they'll think I'm out here cheating on Jason, when it was his ass that was the one cheating.

The children were already dressed and sitting in the den. "Good morning you two. I see you're both ready for church already. Have you eaten breakfast already?" I asked. "Yes ma'am. Mommy you going to church with us this morning?" Myra asked. "I'm going to church baby but I'm driving this morning." I said. "Why you're not going to church with us, like you use to?" Myra asked. "Myra, stop asking Mama all these questions. You know Mama don't ride with Daddy anymore." Jay said. "Okay, I'm glad you're going to church because you stopped going Mommy." Myra said.

I walked over and kissed Myra on her forehead. "You're too smart for your own good sweetheart." I said, as Myra started smiling. "Jay, you look handsome this morning." I said, hugging him. "Thanks Mom. You know I have to look good for the girls." Jay said, rubbing his non-existing mustache, he so desperately wants to have. "Oh I see. Don't you be like your Daddy. You know he loves all the ladies too, even when he should only be loving just one." I said, noticing that Jason just walked in the kitchen when I said that.

Jason acted like he didn't hear me but I could care less if he did or not. "You look nice. Are you going to church or going out again?" Jason asked, in a sarcastic tone. "I'm going to church. I thought about what you said about informing our church members that way when and if they see me out, they won't be thinking, I'm a hypocrite, conniving, lying, cheating, fake first lady." I said.

Jason just stared for a few minutes but didn't say anything. I walked in the kitchen where he was standing, only because I didn't want the children to hear what I had to say. "Is everything good with your apartment now?" I asked. "Yes it is." Jason said. "Good, because I was going to tell you that you need to leave today because you had long enough to get everything straight," I said. "You're right. Thank you for allowing me to stay here for as long as I did." Jason said. "It's okay. I'm glad I was able to help." I said.

Jason came closer to me, as if he was about to whisper something in my ear. "Jannice, what are you going to say to the members?" Jason asked, with a frightened look on his face. "What do you mean? You want to know if I'm going to tell them the truth about everything that happened between us and why we got a divorce?" I asked, looking at him with my hands on my hips. "Well yes. They don't need to know all our business," Jason said. "Why not? You put all those other women in our business," I said. "Please don't do that Jannice. I know I've hurt you but this is my livelihood. This is how you're going to get your child support and alimony." Jason said.

I burst out laughing. "Jason, you're going to pay me my child support and alimony one way or the other. So with the church paying you or your other job, I'm going to get it either way. Because I doubt if you want the children to come visit you locked up." I said. "Don't worry, I'll pay what I'm supposed to pay," Jason said. "Good. I guess I'll see you in church," I said, grabbing my car keys off the kitchen counter.

I pulled up on the church parking lot and just sat in my car for a few minutes. It's eleven o'clock so I grabbed my purse and walked inside the church. I can't believe I'm about to cut all ties with Red Hill church. I've met some great friends, families, and just genuine people here and now I have to say goodbye to them all. "Damn Jason, why couldn't you have just been a good husband to me like I tried being a good wife to you. Now here I am face to tell these people that we're getting a divorce, putting them up in our business.

I closed my eyes and prayed to God to give me a sense of peace to do this. This is the exact closure that I need to move on with my life. I looked at my watch and it was five minutes after eleven. I sat in my car for another fifteen minutes to get my thoughts together before walking in. This had to be done and I started walking to the side of the church. I opened the side door and walked inside. I immediately saw Deacon Henry standing in the hallway. "Hey there first lady." Deacon Henry said, as he extending his hand towards me. "Hey Deacon Henry." It's good to see you this morning." I said. "Good to see you as well." Deacon Henry said. I walked inside and sat beside two of the church mothers on the first row. They both hugged me tightly and I immediately felt the tears came rushing down my face.

I know this is going to be hard to say my goodbyes but it has to be done. My heart was pounding as if it was about to jump out of my body. Jason stood on the pulpit and looked over the congregation. "Good morning Red Hill. Today is the day that the Lord has made, let us rejoice and be glad in it. Church, my wife has something to say this morning so please give her your undivided attention." Jason said.

I walked up on the podium and looked over the congregation. The tears came rushing down my face. "Good morning Red Hill. I'm not going to be before you long, I just had something I wanted to say to you all. I want you all to know that I considered it to be an honor and my pleasure to have served as your first lady for eight years, but today will be my last day with you all. My husband and I just got a divorce and I will be leaving the church for good

I love you all and I pray that you all will continue to be bless in good health as well as wealth. Keep God first in your life. Love on each other and continue to pray with and for your family. Continue to keep my children and our family in your prayers. Thank you all Red Hill and continue to be bless." I said, as I waved to everyone one last time before I headed out the door.

As I drove out the parking lot, I stopped in the middle of the street to look at the church one last time. I served here as first lady for eight years of my life. Farewell Red Hill. I love you all.

CHAPTER

22

Our First time

It's been a month now since Jason moved out the house and I told my final goodbyes to the church. I had a few mixed feelings about looking in their faces as I stood in the pulpit. I saw a lot of the women and children crying and it tore at my heart but I knew it was the right thing to do.

Jason moved the rest of his things out the house and told me he regrets it all and how sorry he is for everything he's put me and the kids through. I told him I forgive him but I know I had to forgive him for me because if I didn't, his betrayal would tear me up and probably destroy me down the line. People don't realize that the forgetting and moving on part is way harder than the forgiveness part. I'm still a work in progress but I'm trying. I'm at a place now in my life that I can at least look at him and not want to punch him in the face.

Things have been good at work. Adrienne told everyone that I would be the new principal and that she was leaving the school and would be the new superintendent. A few people acted like they were happy for both Adrienne and I but we knew they were only pretending. That's one thing about jealousy, it comes in many different forms, but I'm thankful that God has given me the sense and knowledge to be able to see it for what it is and not be blind to it.

I've been in my position now as the new principal and I felt I'm making some good progress, learning and trying to have a good working relationship with all the faculty and staff at the school.

I just got off from work and was heading home for a bit. Ricardo invited me to come over to his place tonight for dinner. He told me he had something special planned for us tonight. I hope tonight will be the night that we do the do. It's been almost three months since a sister had some and I'm way overdue for some hot lovemaking. I sure hope Ricardo sex is as fine and as good looking as he is.

I sat down on the couch and before I knew it, I fell asleep. I decided to take a quick nap so I wouldn't be tired tonight. I called Adrienne up to see if she could watch the kids. We talked about what Ricardo and I had planned tonight so she was ready to watch the kids. I told her I'll have a duffle bag ready for them in case I need them to spend the night but If I come by tonight to get them then she'll know it didn't go well. Adrienne laughed and told me she hopes it works out for me.

I went and jumped in the shower to get ready for dinner at Ricardo's house. Tonight would be my first time invited over to Ricardo's house. I text Adrienne and told her the children was ready and so was I. She texted back with laughing emoji's and told me I was good and crazy and that she was almost here. I went and got the kids and they sat in their rooms until Adrienne got here.

I heard the car door closed and then the car horn. I went and got the kids and brought them to the car. Adrienne got out the car and hugged the kids and told them to get in the car. I hugged the kids before they got in the car. Adrienne walked towards me with a wicked smile on her face. "Look at you all ready and shit. With your nasty ass," Adrienne said laughing. "Don't be hating on me because I'm about to get me some," I said, laughing. "Well have fun and I'll plan for the kids to spend the night if you get lucky." Adrienne said. "Shit, I sure hope I do. A sister need to get her some." I said, laughing. "I bet you do," Adrienne replied, shaking her head. "Have fun," Adrienne said, hugging me.

I texted Ricardo and told him I was ready to come over. He texted me his address and I got in the car and headed over. I pulled up in Ricardo's driveway and I must say his house is absolutely stunning. His house is huge and it made me questioned if Ricardo was really out of the drug business all together.

I knocked on the door and Ricardo came to the door, in a tan linen suit. He looked extremely nice in his linen suit. He had his dread out, which I've never seen them out before. "Hey beautiful." Ricardo said, as he hugged me and kissed me on the lips. "Come on in sweetheart." Ricardo said, as he took my hand and led me inside his home.

Ricardo and I sat down in his den. I looked around his house and it was definitely beautiful. Ricardo, you have a beautiful house." I said. "Thank you baby. It was definitely worth selling drugs for huh?" Ricardo said, laughing. I didn't think his comment was funny at all. "Baby, it's just a joke," Ricardo said. I gave him a half ass smile.

Ricardo stood up and reached his hand out. I reached for his hand as he pulled me up and he hugged and kissed me deeply. "I'm so glad you came over." Ricardo said. "I'm glad you invited me." I replied. "Are you hungry, because everything is done." Ricardo said. "Sure." I said. "Okay, great. The bathroom is around the corner on the right, so you can fresher up in there." Ricardo said.

I went to the restroom to washed my hands and I couldn't help but staring at the beautiful decorations he had in his bathroom. His bathroom was dark chocolate brown and orange. I could tell a woman decorated his house because it was just a little too elegant for a man's taste. Maybe he just has an eye for nice things and color coordination.

I walked back in the den where Ricardo was sitting, waiting for me to return. "Are you ready to eat?" Ricardo asked again. "I am," I replied. "Let's go into the dining room and I'll fix your dinner." Ricardo said. "Okay." I replied.

I sat down at the dining room table and texted Adrienne, Ricardo's address. This is something that we all do, if we spend the night or going to a man's house for the first time. You can never be too careful these days. I sent it only to Adrienne since she was the only one that knew that I was coming to Ricardo's house. "Jannice, what would you like to drink? I have cranberry juice, water, sweet tea, and lemonade." Ricardo said. "Sweet tea sounds good." I said. "Well sweet tea it is." Ricardo said.

Ricardo brought our dinner to the table on a tray. "Wow, the food looks delicious." I said. "Oh, I hope you say that after you taste it." Ricardo said, laughing. "I sure hope so." I replied, joining in with his laughter. Ricardo made rice, gravy, fried pork chops and stem broccoli.

Ricardo grabbed my hand and said grace. It was nice to see that he has some kind of relationship with God at least. We had the best conversation as we enjoyed dinner. I shared with him about my new position as principal and how excited I am about it. He congratulated me and then he asked why I didn't been tell him about it. I told Ricardo that I wanted to wait and see him face to face to share it with him. He smiled and told me that was understandable. Plus, I told him I had a lot going on with getting Jason out my house for good. He acted like he understood but I don't think he did. Ricardo has to realize that I haven't been on a date with another person other than my husband, in over twelve years. This is still new to me. It's a lot that I have to get use to again.

After dinner, Ricardo and I went into the kitchen and washed the dishes together and then we walked in the living room. Before we sat down, Ricardo grabbed me by the waist and kissed me deeply. His lips were very soft and felt so good as his lips touched mine. We definitely had chemistry and it was something that I never felt before, not even with Jason.

Ricardo held me in his arms, rubbing my skin as if he was mesmerized by the softness of it. "Baby, I want to make love to you." Ricardo said, in a sexy whisper. At first I wanted to dive straight on top of him and rip every thread of his clothes off, but I know I had to act like a lady, even though my ass was horny as shit and I was well overdue for some. I still didn't want him thinking I was a thirsty slut either, so I proceeded with caution. "I want you to make love to me too." I said, kissing him on the neck and back around to his lips.

Ricardo took my hand and lead me to his bedroom upstairs. Ricardo had a big king size bed with a zebra print comforter. I removed my clothes and Ricardo removed his clothes as well. Ricardo's body was absolutely perfect as we both stood there admiring each other from head to toe. Ricardo touched my breast and then took it into his mouth. I bit down on my lip as chills went straight up my spine. "A sister about to get her some.

A sister about to get her some." I sang over and over in my head, as a smile displayed on my face.

I was so turned on that I could explode right here. I took my hand and reached for Ricardo's manhood that was fully erected. Ricardo placed me on top his bed and then he climbed on top of me. I know he's about to taste my insides because just the feel and taste of lips, I know he could eat me out like I was some strawberry sundae and he was about to devour me. I know I definitely wouldn't be able to sustain myself then.

Ricardo reached in his nightstand and pulled out a condom and slid it on. "Damn, I guess a sister isn't going to be devour like a sundae then. I was a little disappointed but maybe the sex will be so good that it will not matter that he didn't taste my spot. But if he's going to be my man, that's definitely some shit he will have to change, or else it won't be a next time, because I like to be slurped and turned the fuck out.

Ricardo slid inside me all damn rough and I moaned out. "Damn." I guess his ass doesn't know anything about being gentle or anything. He was now inside me for a few seconds and after getting myself relaxed after he just tried to bull dozier his shit inside me, I was starting to enjoy it. Ricardo had his little stroke game going on, as I was just starting to throw it back to him a little. "Oh damn baby! Damn baby, I'm about to nutt!" Ricardo yelled. "All fucking ready!" I yelled. "Yes! Yes! Yes! Ah fuck!" Ricardo yelled as he started shivering, acting like someone just threw a bucket of ice cubes on top of him.

I looked at this fool as he turned over and it seems like in less than a minute, his ass started snoring. "Are you fucking serious!" This fool acted like he just laid it down and didn't do shit. Three damn minutes if that, is that what I have to look forward to every time we have sex? I got up and grabbed my damn clothes to get dressed. Ricardo didn't even notice I wasn't in bed beside him. I got dressed and went to the den to grab my damn keys and my purse.

I started driving down the highway and I couldn't believe a man as fine and sexy as Ricardo, couldn't fuck worth two damn cents. Three damn minutes, I swear I take longer than that to take a damn piss and wipe myself. "Man Shit! I know damn well I didn't waste a perfect goodnight, where I could've been home watching "Golden Girls," then here with this damn three-minute man. Damn, I can't even describe the way I'm feeling right now. I know I have some brand new batteries at the house so I guess I'm going back in the little box in the top of my closet to put me right to sleep

CHAPTER

23

I Can't Tell You

I arrived at work and went to the cafeteria go get some apple juice to eat my sausage biscuit with. The tardy bell just rung for all the children to be in class. I finished eating my breakfast and I started walking towards my office, when I thought I saw a student, peaking around the corner.

I took a double look because I saw one of the boys, ran into the boy's restroom. All the children should be in class by now. I knocked on the door or the boy's restroom and pushed it open. "Hello. Who's in here?" I asked. "No one, said anything but one of the stalls were closed. I looked under the stall but didn't see anyone standing up. I walked towards the stall door and saw someone standing up on the toilet through the crack in the door. "Who is this? Open this door!" I yelled.

The door opened and Cameron came out the stall. "Cameron, what are you doing in here? You're supposed to be in class." I said. "Mrs. Davis, I was about to go to class." Cameron said. I held Cameron by his shoulders, because I could tell something was going on with him. "Ouch!" Cameron yelled out. "What's wrong?" I asked. I took Cameron's jacket off and looked at his right shoulder. He had red welts all over his right shoulder. I pulled his shirt up from the back and his entire back had bruises and welts all over him.

I couldn't believe what I was looking at. "Cameron, walk with me to my office." I said. The last thing I needed was for someone to come in the boy's restroom and see me pulling Cameron's shirt up. Some people would probably take this the wrong way.

Cameron came inside my office and I closed the door. I sat at my desk and Cameron sat down in the chair across from me. I looked at Cameron and it was obvious that he looked scared, nervous, and upset all at once. "Cameron, did your mom do this to you?" I asked. "No she didn't do this." Cameron said. "Then who did this Cameron?" I asked. "Mrs. Davis, I fell down the stairs and skinned my back up." Cameron said. "Cameron, sweetheart, those bruises and welts on your back, didn't come from you falling down the stairs. Someone has been hurting you." I said.

Cameron started crying hysterically. I came and sat beside him and placed my hand on his back. "Cameron, please tell me who did this to you?" I asked. "Was it your mother?" I asked for the second time. "No Mrs. Davis, it wasn't my mom. My mom loves us all." Cameron said. "Okay, then who was it?" I asked again. "Mrs. Davis, it was my stepfather. Last night my mother asked me to wash the dishes and I told her I was coming. I must not came fast enough for my stepfather, so he came to my room with his belt and started whipping me. He hit me, wherever he could." Cameron said, wiping his eyes.

I took a bottle of water out my mini fridge and gave him one. Cameron opened the water and drunk about half of it. "Cameron, this isn't the first time this has happened, has it?" I asked. "No. He beats me at least about three times a week. It could be the simplest thing too. I remember one night around eight o'clock, I wasn't done with my homework. He told me I must have been in my room goofing off since I wasn't finished yet. So he beat me for that and made me go to bed, without finishing my homework." Cameron said.

I know Cameron wasn't going to like what I had to say but I have to tell him. "Cameron, I promise you that your stepfather will never hurt you again but you do know what I have to do next right?" I said. "Call the police?" Cameron asked, looking even more scared. "Yes and child protective services. They will immediately remove you from the house." I said.

Cameron nodded his head. "Mrs. Davis, I don't want anything to happen to my mom but I can't stay there anymore. I'm afraid my stepfather is going to kill me and my mom." Cameron said. I immediately felt the tears in my eyes for what was happening to Cameron and his mom. No child should be going through what he's going through.

I picked up the phone and called Adrienne immediately. "Hey girl. You won't believe where I am?" Adrienne said, sounding all excited. "Where?" I asked. "I'm here at your school, about to walk to your office. So your timing of calling me was just right." Adrienne said, laughing. "Adrienne, please hurry up in my office. I have an emergency." I said. "Oh damn Jannie. I'm on my way." Adrienne said, hanging up the phone. "Lord, if it's never been a time that I was glad to hear from Adrienne, that would be now." I said to myself.

I heard Adrienne's voice outside talking to Ms. Laura, the secretary. I stuck my head outside my office door. "Hey, Adrienne. Come on back. Ms. Laura it's okay." I said. Adrienne walked in my office and I closed the door behind her. "Hey girl." Adrienne said, giving me a quick hug. "Hey Adrienne." I said. "Hey Cameron. How are you?" Adrienne asked. "I'm not good." Cameron said, drying his eyes. "Lord, Jannie what's wrong and why is Cameron in here?" Adrienne asked.

I know this situation was about to go south really quickly and Cameron's life would no longer be the same. "Adrienne, Cameron told me that his stepfather has been abusing him and his mother." I said. "Cameron, can you stand up for me?" I asked. Cameron stood up. "Cameron is it okay that I show Ms. Williams your back?" I asked.

Cameron had tears in his eyes but he nodded his head, giving me his permission. I pulled Cameron's shirt up for Adrienne could see what his horrible stepfather did to him. Adrienne put her hand over her mouth. "Jannie, oh my God! God no! Not a child! Not a freaking child! Adrienne screamed. "Jannice, you have to call the police and CPS, right now." Adrienne said.

I picked up the phone and called 911 and told the dispatcher that I needed a few police officers to come to Tryon Elementary School. The dispatcher asked me what was the reason and when I told her she informed me she was sending three police officers over. I thanked the dispatcher and then I called CPS and told them the situation as well. A man said that someone would be up there shortly.

I know I should call Ricardo and inform him of what was going on. Ricardo was furious and said he was on his way. I don't know if Ricardo was furious about me calling him after I called the police and CPS or that I should've called him instead of even contacting them. Either way my main priority is keeping Cameron safe and that's it.

CHAPTER

24

The Glow

The police arrived about ten minutes ago and then CPS. Ricardo called me back and ask me to tell CPS to please wait until he get to the school because he was on his way. I informed Ms. Collins and she said as long as he was on his way, she would wait for him. Adrienne and I were out her trying to answer all the questions that the police asked us. Cameron tried answering the police and Ms. Collins questions as well until he started crying again. I can only imagine how scary all this must be for him.

Adrienne and I stepped aside to talk for a few minutes. "Jannie, you might have some issues with Ricardo ass for you calling the police and CPS." Adrienne said. "I know Adrienne and he bet not act a damn fool either, otherwise the police can take his ass to jail to." I said.

The police was waiting for Ricardo to get here and Cameron was sitting in the CPS car. I asked the caseworker Ms. Collins if Ricardo can take Cameron home with him instead of him going to a facility tonight. She said yes he could take him but they will have to start an investigation the next day but if Ricardo can't be with him to watch him then he can't go back with him. I hope that doesn't happen but I don't regret calling the police or CPS for one damn minute.

Ricardo pulled up and parked on the side of the building. He got out the car with an angry look on his face and he walked passed Adrienne and I, as if he didn't see us standing here. I guess he's really upset.

Ricardo was able to take Cameron home with him. He told him to wait in the car as he walked over towards us. "Hello Ladies." Ricardo said. "Hey there." We both said. "Jannice, can I speak to you please?" Ricardo asked. "Sure," I said. "Adrienne, excuse me for a second." I said. "Sure, I'll be over here talking to the police officers." Adrienne said.

I walked over by the car where Ricardo was standing. "Look Jannice, why didn't you call me before you called the police?" Ricardo asked. "Because it's my job to call the police and CPS, to assist with this." I said. "Well, you should've called me first." Ricardo said. "Look, I didn't have to call you at all. I'm only supposed to call the police and CPS, and that's it. So me calling you was only a curtesy call. I didn't have to do that. So if you can't understand that, then that's your problem. So if there's nothing else you have to say other than this, then I'm done talking about this. I've said all I'm going to say about this subject." I said, walking off.

I went back over to where Adrienne was standing, talking to the police. "Is everything okay?" Adrienne asked. "Yes." I said. "Well good." Adrienne said. "Officer what's going to happen now?" I asked. "Well we're about to leave and go pick up Fredrick Moore from his job. Cameron's uncle told us where he works. Ricardo James will have to bring Cameron for a custody hearing tomorrow morning at ten o'clock, so the court can decide what they're going to do with Cameron. If Cameron is going to stay with Mr. James or they're going to place him with someone else, until his mom has a stable place to live. Either way, Cameron won't be going back to that home again." The officer said. "Good." I said.

I was glad to hear that because Cameron definitely doesn't need to go back in that kind of environment again and I hope his mother gets out that abusive home as well. I hope Cameron's stepdad, stays locked up forever.

Adrienne and I decided to have an early lunch since we had a wild morning with Cameron's situation. We decided to go to "Golden Coral." I know I didn't want a big huge lunch so I decided on getting a salad. Adrienne and I ate from the buffet.

I looked at Adrienne's face across from me and she looked so happy. She had such a glow that looked beautiful on her. I couldn't help but to smile. Adrienne noticed I was smiling and she stretched her eyes at me. "Jannie, why are you smiling at me?" Adrienne asked. "Because of that bright glow that you have on your face. It looks good on you and Lord knows you deserve some happiness for a change." I said. "Yes, I have a reason to smile now. Nicolas and I are really enjoying ourselves and I look forward to spending more time with him." Adrienne said. "I'm so glad to hear that." I said.

Adrienne and I finished our lunch and I knew it was time for me to be getting back to work. "How are you liking your new job?" I asked. "I love it. I don't have to stay at one school the entire day. I can move around every other day or every day if I want to. Adrienne said. "I'm glad you like it." I said. "I do. What about you and your new position as being the new principal? Is it everything you hoped it would be?" Adrienne asked. "It is Adrienne and I wouldn't trade it for the world. Now you know I'm still getting a little snickering and stares every now and then from the staff but that's to be expected." I said. "Yes it is. You just have to ignored their dumb asses." Adrienne said.

Adrienne and I walked to our cars. "Girl, I have to tell you about the other night with Ricardo." I said. "You two finally did it?" Adrienne asked. "Yes but trust me, this is a "wine and dine," night. If I tell you about it now, I might as well take the rest of the day off." I said. "Damn Jannie, it was that bad?" Adrienne asked. "Trust me, you don't know the half of it." I said, as we laughed.

CHAPTER

25

I WILL NOT APOLOGIZE

Today was a day from hell. I guess no one said that being the principal would be a piece of cake because Lord knows it's not. I had to call the police, CPS and Ricardo about Cameron this morning. Ricardo had the audacity to act like this was all my fault to get the police and CPS involved. I told him I was doing my job and I'm not apologizing to him or anyone else about what I did. Cameron's safety was my only concern at this time.

I grabbed my briefcase and was heading out the door. I can't wait to get home to soak my body in my hot tub, while drinking a glass of wine. Today has been a damn day and I'm glad my work day is over with.

I took my car keys out my purse before I got to my car and I spotted this black woman walking towards me. It's Cameron's mother Everlyn and she looked upset. I had my hand on my mace that's on my car keys in case I had to give Everlyn a damn beat down. Everlyn and I are classmates but we never really talked in school. We just were in different social groups. Everlyn has always had a reputation as "a bad, fast girl," in school but if she trying to roll up on me, she better know what the hell she's doing.

Everlyn walked towards me with a smirk on her face. "If it aint little uppity Ms. Jannice Rogers. Oh excuse me, I mean Mrs. Jannice Rogers Davis, but then again it might be Jannice Rogers again since you and Pastor are now divorce." Everlyn said, looking a hot mess and laughing. "Hello Everlyn. How are you?" I asked. "Don't you hello Everlyn me. Look what the hell you did to my family?" Everlyn said, getting closer and closer towards me.

I swear I'm not in the mood for this damn hood rat right now but if she wants some heat, I'm ready to bring it three times harder. "Everlyn, look, I didn't do anything to your family. Your son was lurking around in the boy's restroom and when he saw me, he ran back in there trying to hide from me. I took Cameron by his shoulders and when I did he moaned out as if he was in pain. I asked him what was wrong with him and he said he had fell down the stairs. I pulled up Cameron's shirt and that's when I saw all those welts and bruises all over his back. I pulled out my phone and showed Everlyn the pictures of his bruises that I took.

Everlyn took my phone and kept swiping to the right to see the pictures. "Oh my God! Jannice, Fredrick didn't mean to do that." Everlyn said, defending the bastard. I nearly lost my damn mind on her dumb ass. I walked up on her like I was a real damn gangster. "Everlyn if you defend that bastard, I'll beat your damn ass myself. How dare you let that man beat up on your child like that. Your husband is a damn grown ass man, Cameron is a child. You're the one that is supposed to protect him and keep him safe, not sit there and watch your husband beat him like that.

Everlyn dropped her head in shame, when I said that. "You knew Fredrick was abusing Cameron. You've seen him snatched him up or something haven't you?" I asked. "Okay, maybe I did see him yell at him a few times or he might have whipped him a few times when he got out of hand." Everlyn said. "Okay Everlyn but if he hits on you, how could you not think he wouldn't hit your son?" I asked. "Jannice, I never told you that he hits me." Everlyn said. "Everlyn, look at you? You're a beautiful and strong lady and you're always been, but hiding behind your black eyes and your own bruises, doesn't show me or anyone else how strong you are. You know your husband has an anger problem and takes it out on you and Cameron, so don't act like you didn't know he was abusing Cameron, because you did. You might not have known it was quite this bad but you knew." I said.

Everlyn, seem as though she was apologetic for knowing what was happening to her son instead of acting like she was unaware of what was going on. "Everlyn, I don't and will not apologize for calling the police or CPS because that's my job. I'm sure if the shoe was on the other foot and you saw my son, who is the same age as Cameron, you would've done the same thing and I would expect you to do so. Now if you're looking for someone to blame about calling the police and CPS then you should blame yourself for putting me in a position to have to do that and trust me, I would do it again and in your face. I care about all my students and that will never change." I said.

Everlyn started crying uncontrollable. I came closer to her to try and console her. "Look Everlyn, if you ever want to get out that marriage and find a place, then I can possibly help you with that but not until you're ready. I can't help you unless you're willing to admit that there's a problem." I said.

Everlyn looked like she was finally done with defending her husband and now concern about saving her and Cameron's life and get away from him for good.

I reached in my pocket and handed Everlyn a business card. "You have to let me know when you're ready to be done with your husband and ready to take control back from him. So you can get you and your children's life back together, then call me. If not then go on about your life but again, I will not apologize for what I did, because if I had to do it all over again, I would do the same thing. It's not our children's job to protect us, It's our job as parents to protect our children." I said, as I got inside my car and drove away.

CHAPTER

26

Right time, Right Place

Today was a much better day today. I texted my girls and told them it was another wine and dine night. The both gave me a thumbs up. I texted back and told them six o'clock. They both agreed. I ran to Publix to get a fruit tray, twenty-five wings, a large container of potato salad and a bottle of wine. I need to wine and dine with my girls, while we talk shit to each other and about our lives. The cashier was about to ring up my stuff, when I happened to look at another line and I couldn't believe who I saw. It was Ricardo and some young lady and they were looking quite comfortable together.

I didn't say anything as the lady cashier rung up my items. I continued looking over at Ricardo and his little friend. The lady was actually beautiful. She's a brown-skinned lady, with a short haircut and medium size. The lady was laughing and hitting Ricardo on the arm, as if he was teasing her or something. "Ma'am, ma'am," the cashier said, that caused me to jump. "I'm sorry ma'am. I didn't mean to scare you but your total is seventy-five dollars even." The cashier said.

I paid with my credit card and I grabbed my two bags and was heading out the door but as I stood at the door of Publix, I decided to go back and confront this bastard and let him know he was seen.

I walked towards them as Ricardo grabbed their bags and was about to walk out the door. "Hey there Ricardo." I said. Ricardo and the young lady turned around to face me. Ricardo quickly took that smile off his face. "Hey Jannice. How are you?" Ricardo asked. "I'm fine. Hello, I'm Jannice and you are?" I asked, extending my hand towards her. "Hello, I'm Rachel." The woman said, as she shook my hand with a smile. "You're so beautiful. Are you Ricardo's girlfriend?" I asked. "No. I'm his fiancé." Rachel said. "Wow fiancé. Really Ricardo? You never told me you had a fiancé when you asked me out for the first time last month. You didn't tell me you had a fiancé when we slept together for the first time a few days ago. Wow, and I thought you were different. You're just like the rest of these other guys, a big ass liar. Well Rachel, I hope you know you have a player on your hands because he definitely tried to run game on me, by telling me he was single and was looking for a good woman." I said.

Rachel, grabbed her chest and did a double look back at Ricardo. "Rick is this true? We're you two involved?" Rachel asked Ricardo. "No baby. She's lying. "Ricardo said. "Rachel, can I ask for your phone number? I'll forward you our messages and all the pictures he's sent me." I said.

Rachel gave me her phone number and I forward her all our text messages. "Rachel, I'm sorry to have to be the one to tell you this, but I'm glad I know now, because I can now move on with my life. This fool isn't worth it. Ricardo, take care of yourself and please lose my phone number." I said, about to walk off. "Oh Rachel, one more thing, I sure hope Ricardo last longer with you then he did with me while having sex. Girl, because as soon as he got the condom on and stroke two or three times, four minutes later he nutted. Then his ass rolled over and went to sleep, so I hope you get a little longer than what I got. Take care Rachel. You seem like a beautiful person, inside and out." I said, as I walked out the store.

I put my things in the back seat of my car and drove off. I must admit this wasn't what I was expecting from Ricardo. I thought he was going to be my knight and shining armor, instead he turned out to be a damn thorn in my damn side.

I started driving and I realize that I lost myself once, trying so desperately to be love, even though I wasn't looking for love. I think I've always been the type that love hard when I start falling for someone and that's when I get hurt, all over again.

I'm sure Jason isn't haven't any problems meeting people, since he's been meeting people the entire time since we've been married. I hope he finds what he's looking for because I definitely wasn't it, even though I tried my best to make our marriage work. I tried being spontaneous but that still wasn't enough for him.

I'm so glad I was in the right place and at the right time, otherwise I probably would've never found out the truth about Ricardo. I wanted to just beat myself up for allowing myself to think that there could be a happily ever after between us. I'm such a fool for believing that true happiness really does exist, because clearly it doesn't.

CHAPTER

27

Wine and Dine

I just got home and started preparing for "Wine and Dine." I told Jay and Myra to stay in their rooms until "Wine and Dine," is over with. We never allow the children to be around when we have our little event and start drinking. There's no telling what any of us might say, especially when we get a few drinks in us.

The girls definitely need to know what a sister has been going through, just within this damn week. I have so much weighing on me that I could actually write my first autobiography and name it "Jannice tells it all." Shit if Jada Smith can do it, then I should be able to as well. With a toxic marriage and thinking I met someone only to later find out that they're both lying, cheating bastards is an understatement.

I tried to ignore all the negative thoughts that was going through my head to focus on my "Wine and Dine." I pulled the wings out the oven after reheating it and adding a little seasoning. Everything was set up with the fruit tray, wings, potato salad and devil eggs and the wine was on the table

I sat down and looked at my phone. I had six missed phone calls from Ricardo. "What the hell is he calling me for? I hope this fool doesn't think, I going to entertain his lying ass any further. Ricardo James is a part of my past. A little fling and judging by his sex, shit a sister isn't missing anything.

The doorbell ranged, snapping me out of my stroll down memory lane, that I just went on thinking about the two men that recently hurt me.

I went to the door and both Adrienne and Sharese were at my door with a bottle of wine in their hands. "Hey there." I said, as I hugged them both and invited them inside. Sharese and Adrienne immediately got comfortable by taking off their shoes and walking around barefooted.

We all ate and then we dived into our wine and started our discussions about what was going on in our lives. It seems like I always have the most shit to share. I guess Sharese and Adrienne's lives are pretty boring right about now.

Sharese said how much she's falling for Scott and how he's took her on about three trips, since they started dating. Sharese said that Scott's family were really wealthy people but she got the impression that they don't like that he's dating outside his race. Sharese said that Scott hasn't mentioned to her about when he wanted her to meet his family so she knows it had to do with her being black. Sharese hope to meet his family one day but she's not about to kiss no one's ass to get along with them because of their stupid views.

Adrienne and I both agreed with what Sharese said. I asked Sharese do she see marriage in the near future and she burst out screaming "yes." It's good to see how happy she is and I wish nothing but the best for her and Adrienne.

Adrienne shared that she was loving her new job as the school superintendent. She said most the staff and teachers were warming up to her and giving their prospective of the school and ways they think the school could improve. Adrienne said how she and Nicolas made dinner together and how nice it was. She said Jermaine and Nicolas were warming up to each other a little better now, then they first met. Adrienne said that Jermaine asked Nicolas all kinds of questions, like if he's been married before or have any children, and what he did for a living.

Adrienne said Nicolas answered all Jermaine's questions but he told Adrienne later on that Jermaine had every right to ask him the type of questions he asked. Nicolas told her that for so long it was just her and Jermaine in each other's lives and Jermaine, just wanted to know if he was going to stick around and not hurt his mom.

Sharese and I told Adrienne that Jermaine asked all the right questions as well. I told her to give it some time and those two will be the best of friends. Adrienne laughed and said, she can't wait for that to happen.

I took another sip of my wine and took a deep breath. "Damn, you got that much to share?" Adrienne asked. "Shit, you don't know the half of it." I said. Sharese and Adrienne turned all the way around in their seats to face me. "I swear, yall love gossip too much." I said. "Hell yeah and Jannie, no one can tell a damn story like your ass can. All I need is some popcorn because you're about to take us on a damn adventure." Sharese said, as we all laughed.

I know they were ready for me to spill my damn guts and I wasn't about to disappoint them. "Well yall Ricardo and I finally had sex." I said. "What! Are you serious!" Adrienne screamed. "Girl, not so loud. You know the kids are up in their rooms." I said. "Oh sorry." Adrienne said. "Look, how was it?" Sharese asked. "Sharese, it was horrible. I've never had sex that bad in all the days of my life. Not even when I was sixteen and I called myself doing it with Terrell Willis. Shit at least Terrell lasted about eight minutes. Ricardo didn't even last five damn minutes." I said. "Just when I was starting to relax to enjoy it, the bastard nutted." I said.

Sharese and Adrienne was nearly on the damn floor laughing. "Stop that yall. It's not that damn funny." I said. "I swear that's a damn shame for someone as fine as Ricardo is, to not even last five damn minutes. Please tell me he lick it before he stick it?" Sharese asked. "Hell no. Not even a damn taste." I said.

Sharese and Adrienne burst out laughing. "Yall play too much." I said, taking another sip of my wine. We finished the other two bottles of wine while I told them about Everlyn and how she approached me. They both remembered Everlyn from high school and how fast she was. They weren't surprised that Everlyn got caught up with her abusive husband because she was always wanting attention in high school and didn't care about what man it came from.

We were all toasted when I finally told them about Ricardo and his fiancé Rachel. Adrienne, fell out on the floor, with her mouth wide open, as if she was shocked. I took the pillow from off my chair and threw it at her head. Adrienne got up laughing. "Jannie, you always seem to have way more shit going on than we do. I swear you keep a sister rolling. I couldn't imagine us not having "Wine and Dine," because there's no telling what we're all going to talk about." Adrienne said. "You damn right." Sharese chimed in.

CHAPTER

28

Can you help me?

I just got home from work and I just reclined back in my recliner. Jason texted me and asked me could he pick the children up from school. I told him that was fine, that way I'll have time to just relax and regroup. There's been a lot going on and with me having a hangover from last night didn't make it any easier for me.

I haven't had any major behaviors since I became the principal. I've heard a few sly remarks but I guess that comes with the job and working with shady ass people. I grabbed the remote and turned on the TV. I started watching "Gunsmoke". It seems as if I've been watching it the entire time but in reality the TV was watching me. I had no idea I was this tired, until I woke my own self up from my snoring.

I got up to use the restroom and to get something to drink. Ricardo has been texting me all day and of course I ignored all his text messages. I have nothing to tell him. Whatever he want to talk about, he better talk it over with his little Rachel.

I sat down at the kitchen table to drink my tea. My phone started ringing. I looked at my phone but didn't recognized the number so of course I didn't answer it. The person called two more times but I still didn't answer the call. I received a text, "Hey Jannice, it's me Everlyn. I need your help.

I dreaded calling Everlyn back but I did, just in case it was an emergency. "Hello," Everlyn said. "Hey Everlyn. What's up?" I asked. "Hey Jannice. I need your help. My husband is out and he came over here, trying to get inside. He knocked down the door and he attacked me. I can't stay here tonight or anymore for that matter." Everlyn said. "Do you think I can stay with you tonight and leave in the morning?" Everlyn asked. "Hell no. You can't stay here. I'll tell you what I can do. I'll get you a hotel room for a week and hopefully you'll decide within that week or what you're going to do." I said.

Everlyn didn't say anything. Maybe she hadn't really thought about it. "Are you still there? That's all I can do." I said. "Okay. That will work then." Everlyn said. "Okay, text me your address and I'll come get you." I said.

Everlyn texted me her address and I grabbed my keys. I don't know why I'm entertaining this shit but she needs my help. I called Adrienne and asked her could she ride with me and I told her I'll tell her all about it when I get there. Adrienne told me she would ride with me but Lord if she knew what I was about to do, she would curse me out and tell me hell no.

I pulled up in Adrienne's driveway and blew the horn. Adrienne came out and jumped in the car. "Hey girl, what's up?" Adrienne asked, as she hit my knee with her fist as we always did growing up. "Girl, where are we going?" Adrienne asked. "It's a surprise." I said. "Okay. I love surprises." Adrienne said. "Your ass isn't going to like this surprise when you find out where we're going." I said to myself.

I drove about fifteen minutes down the road, listening to the GPS. "Jannice, where the hell are we going?" Adrienne asked, as she started looking around in the area at the houses and run down apartments. I could tell her ass was getting agitated so I knew I had to tell her something fast. "Everlyn called me to pick her up. So I told her I will pick her up and take her to a hotel." I said. "Jannice, I know damn well you didn't get me out my damn house to go with you to pick that whore up. If I knew you was going to do that, I would've stayed my ass in my own damn house. Shit, take me back home." Adrienne said. "Adrienne look, we're not far, as soon as I get her, I'll take her to the hotel and I'll take you back home." I said. "Jannice, you have done some crazy ass shit growing up, but this has to be the dumbest thing you have ever done." Adrienne said. "Damn Adrienne, why you being so hard on a sister?" I said. "Jannice, have you ever thought that this could be a damn set up or something?" Adrienne asked. "A set-up?" I replied.

Adrienne shook her head at my question. "Jannie, sweetheart you're a very smart lady but I swear you can have a few Rose Nylund moments at times and this is definitely one of those times. Look, you called the police and CPS on her and her husband. They took Cameron away from them and locked up Everlyn's husband. Now she's calling you telling you she's afraid for her life? Come on Jannie, use your damn brain." Adrienne said.

The more I thought about what Adrienne was saying, the more it made sense to me. "Damn Adrienne. I never thought of that." I said. "Yes Jannie. Revenge is a dangerous thing, especially when you feel like you have nothing else left but to get back at the person that hurt you. Remember how you said how Everlyn approached you when you were going to your car and how scared you were? Now you going to pick her ass up? Please don't take my next statement the wrong way, but you look like a damn fool!" Adrienne said.

I swear this chick has a way with her words and don't give two cents, how it may effect someone's feelings. Adrienne, is going to tell you exactly how she feels and not sugarcoat a damn thing. "I swear you don't sugarcoat nothing do you?" I asked. "Hell no. After thirty years of friendship, Jannie you should be use to this shit by now." Adrienne said, with a smile. "Trust me, I am. If I was a sensitive person, I don't think you and I would still be friends by now. Because you don't care what comes out of your mouth." I said. "Or what goes in it. Trust me Nicolas will agree to that." Adrienne said. "Yuck, with your nasty ass. I don't want to hear all that nasty shit." I said.

Adrienne burst out laughing. "Ah, don't be all jealous, since the last time you had some is when you had Ricardo and you blink your eyes twice, and his ass was done." Adrienne said.

I laugh at Adrienne so damn hard, that I almost ran off the damn road. "Adrienne, I swear I'm going to put your ass out my car." I said. "Well, I'm just trying to make you laugh." Adrienne said. "You're doing too much of that." I said.

The GPS told me to make a right into the apartment complex. I found her apartment and oh my God, it looked like an abandon set of apartments that were condemned. No one should be living here. The building had graffiti all over it with gang signs. The grass looked like it was up to your knees. The apartment windows had rock holes in them as well as boards nailed up to the windows. I can't imagine anyone living like this. I immediately felt sorry that Cameron had to live in these conditions.

I took my cell phone out to call Everlyn, before I parked in one of the spaces. I turned around so I could be facing the way I came in, in case I had to make a quick get a way. "Hello, Everlyn." I'm outside, waiting by your apartment." I said. "Jannice, can you come in and help me with a few of my bags. I have a lot." Everlyn said. "Just grab what you can and we can put it in the trunk." I said. "Come on inside." Everlyn said. "Okay," I replied.

I hung up the phone and was about to get out the car. "Jannice, if you get out this car, talking about you're going to help her with some damn bags, I'll kick your ass myself. You better not get out of this car. And look, don't you see her front door is still attached? That damn girl is trying to set you up." Adrienne said. Adrienne was right. I had no business getting out my car to go inside there and the front door was on her apartment and not kicked down.

We waited for about five minutes and Everlyn hadn't come out yet. I called her again but she didn't answer. Seconds later, she called back and asked if I was coming up to help her. Everlyn, sounded scared as hell, and she was slurring her speech and repeating herself. "No, I'm not coming in there. Just bring your stuff outside." I said. Everly paused for a few seconds, without saying anything. I immediately could tell something was wrong. "Everlyn are you in trouble? Is your husband inside trying to make me come inside?" I asked. "Yes." Everlyn said. "I'll call the police." I said.

I hung up the phone with Everlyn, and jumped when Adrienne scream, scaring the shit out of me." Girl, what!" I yelled. I looked back and saw four black men coming towards my car with a ski mask over their heads and holding guns.

I stepped on the acceleration and hauled ass out the complex. The men came running and then they stopped, when they saw how fast I turned that curve. "Oh shit. I felt like we had just robbed the bank and I was driving the get-a-way car. I looked over and Adrienne was holding her chest as if she was afraid to let go and breathe. "Shit Adrienne, I think you're safe now." I said. "Lord, thank God because if they had got us, I would've gave them a Fred Sandford heart-attack, falling on the ground, shaking and foaming out the damn mouth and all. They wouldn't know if I was having a heart-attack or a damn seizure," Adrienne said, as we both laughed.

I pulled up to Adrienne's house to drop her off. Adrienne looked at me with a serious look on her face. "Jannie, the next time you want to save the damn world, how about you leave me out of it. Shit our ass was almost the ones' that needed saving." Adrienne said. "Girl, I'm done!" I laughed. "Good." Adrienne said. "I swear you my ride-a-die. Because you know Sharese wouldn't have done that in a million years," I said. "Hell no. Sharese would've hung up in your face and wouldn't answer your calls until two day later." Adrienne said. "That's definitely her." I replied, bursting out laughing.

I pulled out of Adrienne's driveway and called the police. I told them I think someone was being held hostage in their apartment. I gave them the address number and the name of the apartment complex and hung up the phone. I did all I was going to do so my job was done.

CHAPTER

29

God's Protection

Lord, I'm so glad it's the weekend. I sat in my room and started watching a movie on Netflix. I wasn't planning on doing anything today. I was into the movie when I saw my cell phone ringing. I looked at the front of my screen and saw it was Adrienne calling. I swear if I didn't piss Adrienne off last night to almost bring her in a dangerous situation, then I would send her straight to my voice mail. I decided to answer her call since I felt like I owed her for what I made her endure last night.

I picked the phone up to answer. "Hey. Good morning my friend." I said. "Good morning Jannie." Arienne replied, sounding sad. "Girl, why you sound so sad? You sound like someone just died," I said. "Someone did die and they were probably going to take us down with them." Adrienne said. "Adrienne, stop talking around in circles and tell me what's happened." I said, getting frustrated with her ass.

Adrienne paused for a few seconds. "Jannie, you remember when we went over to that God forsaken apartment yesterday evening to pick up Everlyn?" Adrienne asked. "Yes, I do" I replied. "Everlyn's husband was inside that apartment waiting on us. He had Everlyn held hostage in there. Everlyn's husband ended up killing her and himself. If we were stupid enough to go inside her apartment, it would probably be four people dead instead of two." Adrienne said.

My mouth dropped and I almost dropped my phone on the floor. "Adrienne, please tell me you're making this up?" I asked. "Yeah I am. I have nothing to do but call you and tell you that two people are dead and it could've been us right?" Adrienne said with an attitude. "Okay, good point. Sorry, I'm just speechless," I said. "I know, that's why I'm going to give you a pass on that crazy question," Adrienne said.

Adrienne started crying on the phone. "I couldn't stand that heifer but I wouldn't wish this kind of death on anyone," Adrienne said. "Adrienne, you never cared for Everlyn at all. Why is that?" I asked, wondering why she despised her so much. "Because she was a slut and would sleep with anyone, just to get what the hell she wanted. I remember in Biology, I tried my best to get an "A" in Mr. Britt's class. I would go home and try to do extra credit and do some of the bonus questions on the test, just to get an extra five or ten points on it. Mr. Britt made sure I never got an "A" or if I did it was a very low "A" like a ninety-four or ninety-five or something but somehow Everlyn always got hundreds on everything.

I wonder why that was because there was no damn way that the girl was smarter than me, but she always had better grades than me. So one day after we got our test back that Mr. Britt graded, Everlyn had to go to the restroom and she left her test on her desk. I grabbed her test and looked over it with my test. Jannie, she had everything wrong but her answers were marked right and up under the correct answer was a line draw under it. I wonder what was Mr. Britt and Everlyn had going on that he was giving her good grades.

So one day I realize I left my Biology book in Mr. Britt's class and I had to go get it because we had a test the next day. I was just getting out of basketball practice so it would've been around five-thirty or so. I went to the class and the door was unlocked but I saw all Mr. Britt's things on top his desk, like his car keys, his lunchbox and his jacket. I wonder why his things were still on his desk but he wasn't in the classroom. I left it alone but once I saw my book, I grabbed it and was heading out the door when I started hearing moaning. Jannie, it was loud moaning, like someone was getting it in, in the laboratory. So of course my nosey ass went back there to investigate and I took my phone out as well. Jannie, Mr. Britt had Everlyn bent over the table fucking her. I recorded it with my phone but the only thing was you couldn't see their faces. So I deepened my voice and called their names out loud, and when they turned around, I knew I had their asses and faces on the video.

Jannie, they had no idea it was me recording them, because I was behind a bookshelf, they just knew they were being recorded. So I closed up my phone, grabbed my Biology book and hauled ass out of the school as fast as I could. So by the time they got their clothes up and came looking for me, I was long gone. I ran all the way home, which wasn't far since I stayed around the corner from the school." Adrienne said.

I listened to what Adrienne said but I wonder if she's telling the truth. Adrienne can embellish a story and make it more then what it really is. "So what did you do with the video?" I asked. "I went to my dad's office that was in the house and emailed the video to Mr. Britt. I had to make up an email because this definitely couldn't be linked back to me, otherwise my ass would be in hot water, but then again who was going to tell it, Mr. Britt or Everlyn? The next morning, I went to Mr. Britt and told him I was the one that sent the video and from here on out, I better be getting freaking one hundreds on everything I take in his class, otherwise I would make it that he would get fired and would never work as a teacher again.

I told Mr. Britt that on the last day of school, I'll come back to his class and I'll delete the video in front of him. He agreed to my terms and I got straight hundreds for the rest of the school term, which boost up my GPA tremendously. But since that day that I caught Mr. Britt and Everlyn in the lab together, I despised that chick, because I knew she would sleep with anyone just to get what she wanted and I knew I had the power to put an end to that but I never told anyone about it, I just deleted the video like I told Mr. Britt that I would. Everlyn never stopped and look what she got in the end. Some things not even sex can get you out of." Adrienne said.

I wonder why Adrienne never told us this story before? "I know I should've told you and Sharese about this but I didn't know how you would look at me for using the video to my advantage to get what I wanted. Yes, I used it to get ahead. Was it wrong? Yes, but what they were both doing was wrong too. So I use the video as my leverage." Adrienne said.

I know I had to say something, trying not to sound judgmental or anything. "I see. I guess we all have to be careful messing with your ass huh? You better not have no videos of my ass bend over no desk or table or anything," I said, laughing.

"Girl please. I would never hurt my girls like that ever. We've been through too much shit together. "Adrienne said. "Yeah, your definitely right about that. Look, we will talk later. Let me get the kids lazy behinds up so they can start their day." I said. "Okay, I'll talk to you later. Kiss the kids for me." Adrienne said. "I sure will and kiss Jermaine for me." I said. "Okay." Adrienne replied.

I hung up the phone with Adrienne. I got on my knees and prayed for Cameron, as well as Ricardo's family. I'm sure glad Adrienne and I didn't go inside that apartment, otherwise we probably would've been dead to. God will always protect his children. For in the time of trouble, he shall hide me in his pavilion, in the secret of his tabernacle. Thank you God for your protection.

CHAPTER

30

Marcus Johnson

I got up off the couch and showered and put some clothes on. The children were up playing their games in their bedrooms. I felt my phone vibrating in my pocket. I looked at it and it was Jason calling. I wonder what he wants.

I answered the phone, even though I didn't want to. "Hello," I said. "Good morning Jannice. How are you?" Jason asked, sounding cheerful this morning. "Good morning Jason. I'm fine. How are you this morning?" I asked, as if I cared. "I'm great. Look, I'm taking the kids to Carowinds this morning and it would be nice. Well let me rephrase that, I would like it if you would come with us. Even though we're not married anymore, we're still a family and it would be nice if we can still do things as a family if you're okay with that?" Jason asked.

I listened to Jason's words and he was absolutely right, we may not be married anymore but we're still a family. "Thank you Jason for the invite and you're right we are still family. Can I have a raincheck on Carowinds please? I had some kind of week. After my promotion at work, I've had quite a few challenges," I said. "Promotion? You got a promotion at work?"

Jason asked, with excitement in his voice. "Yes I did," I said. "Wow, you didn't tell me that. What kind of promotion did you get?" Jason asked.

I wanted to ask Jason, why the hell should I tell him about my promotion, we're not like that or married anymore. What the hell he thinks we're about to be besties or something? "I'm the new principal, Jason." I said. "Congratulations Jannice. You definitely deserve it but what about Adrienne? Wasn't she the principal there?" Jason asked. "Yes she was. She's now the superintendent of the entire district," I said, hoping Jason would get back to the subject he first called me about. "I'm happy for you Jannice. You definitely deserve it. So you're going to take a raincheck about going to Carowinds?" Jason asked. "Yes, I need to rest," I said. "Okay. Tell the kids that I'm on my way." Jason said. "I will," I replied, hanging up the phone.

I got up to get the kids. "Good morning my handsome son." I said. "Good morning my beautiful mother. But Lord Mama, you're not beautiful now. You got your hair standing up all over the place." Jay said, laughing. "Oh boy. Do I look that bad?" I asked. "You sure do. Your hair looks like you were in an explosion." Jay said, laughing. "I know better than to ask you something like that." I said. "That's right, because you know I'm gonna tell you the truth." Jay said. "But I love my Mama with the bad hair though." Jay said, walking over to give me a hug. "I love you to son." I said, returning his hug and kissing him on the cheek.

I heard Myra's little feet, coming down the hallway. "Good morning Mommy. What yall in here talking about?" Myra asked, as she hugged me tightly. "Myra, your brother said my hair looks like an explosion. Do you think so?" I asked. "Yes Mommy and your breath is kicking to. What did you eat this morning sardines?" Myra asked, while Jay burst out laughing. "Oh my God, it must be gang up on Mama day this morning huh?" I said. "No Mommy, it's tell Mommy to get herself together day." Myra said, with her little innocent smile, as she kissed me on the cheek.

I couldn't help from laughing at my children. I swear if no one else in the world loves me, I know they do. I couldn't ask for better children then the ones that I have. "Look, your dad is on his way to take you both to Carowinds. So your ready right?" I asked. "Yes, we are Mama. I came in Myra's room and helped her picked something out for her to wear and ran her bath water for her." Jay said. "Thank you sweetheart. You're such a wonderful son." I said. "Yes, Jay is a good big brother." Myra said, hugging

Jay. "I always want you two to be close like this. Jay, you should always have your sister's back and Myra, you should always have your brother's back. Jay, you protect your sister from those knuckle head little boys that will try to date her, and Myra, you protect your brother when you see a girl stepping to him in a way that she shouldn't be. You both look out for each other." I said. "We will Mom." Jay said. "Good. Now stay up here and I'll let you know when your father gets here." I said. Walking to my room.

I brushed my hair up and put it in a ponytail. The last thing I want Jason to think is that I just let myself go since our divorce. I brushed my teeth since Myra said, my breath smelled like sardines. I sat on the couch in the den and started watching TV. I heard the doorbell rang. I got up and went to the door. "Hello Jannice." Jason, said as he tried to hug me. I quickly stuck my hand out and stepped back. "Hello." I said, extending my hand as he gave me a weird look. "So, we're not over the handshake thing yet?" Jason asked.

I laughed, like he was a comedian. "Jason, am I supposed to run up to you and tongue you down, like we're still married?" I asked. "Yes. That would be nice. I laughed again. "Come on Jason, it wasn't good enough for you then, so why would it be good enough for you now?" I asked.

I went upstairs to get the kids. "Jay and Myra, your father is here." I said, standing by their room. "Okay Mom. Love you," Myra said, hugging me. "Love you too and have fun today." I said, kissing Myra on the cheek. "Mom, we're see you later," Jay said. "Okay baby. Have fun and enjoy." I said. "We will," Jay said, as he hugged me before they headed downstairs.

I waited until the kids walked out the door and then I locked the front door. I decided to get out the house for a little while and go to the park. Some nice sunshine would do me some good.

I grabbed my keys and headed to the park. I pulled up in the parking lot and apparently everyone had the same idea of going to the park today. I walked a few laps and then sat down at the picnic table, watching the children play on the playground. The children were really enjoying themselves as they ran around playing with each other.

The wind felt so good with the sunshine, beaming on my butter-scotched skin. I heard a man's voice called my name. "Who the hell is this calling my name like they're my teacher or something. I turned around and it was Marcus. "How are you doing?" I asked, giving him a hug and a peck on the cheek.

I haven't seen Marcus in forever. Marcus and Jason has been friends for forever. He used to come by the house every now and then to watch the football game with Jason but he stopped coming around like four or five years ago.

Marcus sat down across from me on the picnic table. "So, how have you been?" Marcus asked. "I'm good. Trying to make it I guess. How about you? You look good, like you're been taking care of yourself?" I said. "I'm good and I try to. How are the kids doing?" Marcus asked. "They're good. Keeping me busy," I said, laughing. Marcus joined in with my laughter.

The way Marcus looked at me, I know he was about to ask me about Jason. "I heard about you and Jason. I just have one question to ask you?" Marcus said. "And what is that?" I asked, with an inquisitive look on my face. "What took you so long to leave and divorce him?" Marcus asked.

I was shocked at his question and couldn't believe he asked me that. "So, I guess you've known for a while that Jason has been cheating on me huh?" I asked. "Yes I have. Jannice look, it's nothing that he's told me and you think, we discussed that kind of stuff. The only way I know is that I caught him with the woman at a hotel. Do you remember my ex-girlfriend Monica?" Marcus asked. "Yes, the pretty brown-skinned girl you use to date right?" I asked.

Marcus reached in his pocket and put his cell phone on the table. "Well she used to work at Comfort Inn, in Belmont. She needed a ride to work after she got off her main job. So I took her to work and as I parked for her to go inside, I saw this man that resembled Jason from the back and he was wearing an Atlanta Braves baseball cap. Of course, I had to get a good look at him just to make sure that was him. I even took a picture of his vehicle in front of the hotel along with his license plate. Now you know Jason ass is a good liar so I took a quarter out my pocket and put it up under his windshield wiper, where the rubber part would hold it in place if he drove off. Just so he wouldn't lie his ass out of it." Marcus said.

I had to take deep breaths to calm myself down because I know my blood pressure was rising up higher and higher by the minute, but I continued to listen. "So did you confront him?" I asked. "Yes, I did later on that night. Of course he lied out of it and when I showed him the picture and told him where the quarter was on his windshield, he finally told me the truth. I told him you're a good woman and if he's going to cheat then leave you alone and let you find someone that deserves you." Marcus said. "And what did he say?" I asked. "He told me to mind my own damn business. I told him that I don't condone what he's doing and he's a damn hypocrite. I mean how the hell are you preaching to your members and you're fucking everything that moves." Marcus said.

If Marcus is telling me the truth than it takes a good friend to tell your friend that, especially if you know their doing wrong. "Marcus, why didn't you tell me?" I asked. "Jannice, if I had told you that about your husband and the father of your children, would you have believed me?" Marcus asked. "Probably not, but you could've at least tried." I said. "Jannice, are you still friends with Adrienne and Sharese?" Marcus asked. "Yes the best of friends." I said, proudly. "Okay, so tell me how would you feel if they both knew you were cheating on Jason and because they think Jason's a good person, they told him, how would you feel? Would you ever trust them again, even though you knew what they did was right?" Marcus asked. "Okay. I get your point." I said, knowing Marcus was right.

I had tears in my eyes as I quickly wiped them away. "How could I have been so stupid Marcus? How could I have love a man that didn't love me back to feel that he had to screw other women. I'm a good woman and I deserve better than him." I said. "I know you do. You deserve someone like me that will love you." Marcus said. "Someone like you?" I asked. "Yes. Someone like me. Jannice, I know I may not be as handsome as Jason but I think I'm a handsome man. I don't have a six pack like Jason but I don't have a belly either." Marcus said, as we laughed.

Marcus touched my face and then smiled at me. "Look, I made you smile." Marcus said. "Yes, you did," I replied. "Jannice, I've had the biggest crush on you since forever and when I found out that Jason was cheating on you it crushed me. It crushed me because he has a beautiful, loving, smart, intelligent wife and he's fucking around on you, and I hated him for that. "You deserve a good man and I promise that I'll give you the world or die trying to. Jason and I stopped talking for about four years and I'm really glad. I can't be around anyone like that, that would treat you like that." Marcus said.

I looked at Marcus and his eyes filled with tears. "Jannice, can I have your heart? I promise to do right by it and do right by you? Let me be the man you need. Just give me a chance? Please tell me you'll give me a chance?" Marcus asked. "Can we take things slow? I know we know each other but I want to know if I can trust you with my heart as well as my love?" I asked. "Sure you can." Marcus said, as he stood up and took my face in his hand and kissed me passionately. I welcome his touch as well as his kiss. "You promise to do me right Marcus? Because, Jason bruised me but he didn't break me." I said. "And now it's my job to continue to hold you up and nurse those bruises until they heal completely," Marcus said. Call me stupid but I believe every word that came out of Marcus mouth and I'm ready to take this leap of faith with him.

CHAPTER

31

Mom, Help Us!

I just left the park and was on my way home, when my phone ranged. It was Jay calling. "Hey sweetheart, how are you?" I asked. Jay sounded like he was crying. "Baby, what's wrong?" I asked, as I quickly pulled on the side of the road. "Mom, we're at the hospital," Jay said. "Oh my God Jay. What are you all doing at the hospital? Is it Myra?" I asked. "No Mom. It's Dad. Dad's been shot!" Jay cried. "Oh no! Jay, are you all at CaroMont in Gastonia?" I asked. "No. We're at Novant Health in Charlotte." Jay said. "Okay baby. I'm on my way." I said.

I called both Adrienne and Sharese and told them that Jason was shot. They both said they would meet me at the hospital. It seemed like I got to the hospital in about ten minutes instead of twenty-five. I was praying the entire time that Jason would be alright. Jay didn't say much, other than Jason's been shot, so I don't know how bad it is. I sure hope he'll be okay and pull through.

I reached the receptionist desk. "Hello, ma'am. May I help you?" The receptionist asked. "Hello. My son called me about thirty minutes ago and told me their father was shot." I said. "Oh no ma'am. I'm so sorry to hear that. Let me see what room he's in. What is your husband's name?" The receptionist asked. "It's Jason Davis." I said. "Ma'am, he's in room 482." The receptionist said. "Thank you so much." I said.

I got off the elevator and walked around to the waiting room, where Myra and Jay was sitting. "Mom. Myra screamed, as she and Jay ran to hugged me. I hugged both my children for dear life and the tears came rushing down my face. "Mom, I can't breathe," Myra said. I looked at her and smiled as I kissed her all over her beautiful brown face. "Ah Mom. You know I don't like all that kissing mess." Myra said, smiling. "Are you both okay? I asked, ignoring Myra's comment. "Mom, we're okay now that you're here." Jay said. "Jay, what happened?" I asked. "Mom, we were coming out of CiCi pizza, when this man ran up to us. He told Dad to give him his wallet. Dad, reached in his pocket and threw it on the ground for the man to get it." Jay said.

I could tell Jay was still terrified because he was trembling, as he was talking. "Baby, it's okay. Calm down and finish telling me what happened." I said. "Mom, after Dad gave him the wallet, the man picked up the wallet and Dad punched the man and he fell down. The man then pointed the gun at Dad. Dad grabbed us and tried to put us in the car but the man shot Dad in the back like two times. Dad fell on the ground and the man started running. I grabbed my phone and called 911 and tried doing CPR until the EMS arrived. Once they got to where we were and took over with Dad, I then called you when they loaded him up in the ambulance and told us which hospital they were taking us to. Jay said.

I hugged Myra and Jay again, thanking God that my children were alive and safe and for sparing their lives. A young doctor came out in the waiting room where we were. "Mrs. Davis? Is there a Mrs. Davis here?" The doctor asked.

I jumped up and ran towards the doctor. "Hello, I'm Mrs. Davis," I said. "Hey Mrs. Davis, I'm Dr. Dixon. Your husband just came out of surgery and he's fine. The bullet went straight through his back, just missing his spine. If it was a half an inch over, I would probably be telling you some bad news. Now he's going to need some therapy and he can't stay alone, until he's on his feet. Mr. Davis told me that you two are divorce but do you think you can put up with him for at least a month, otherwise he'll have to go to a rehab facility until, he's able to walk again." Dr. Dixon said.

I swear the last thing that I wanted to hear that Jason died but hell I didn't want to hear this shit either. I was planning on moving forward with my life and definitely not having him in my house. "Shit." I said, out loud. "I know this is a lot to ask Mrs. Davis but he needs you to be his rock right now." Dr. Dixon said. "Hell, I needed him to be my damn rock in our marriage but instead of that, he just became the biggest whore." I said, not realizing that I said that out loud.

Dr. Dixon shook his head at my comment. "It sounds like Mr. Davis took you through a lot with stepping outside of the marriage, which I definitely can't understand why, so if you would like, I can set up his rehabilitation stay with the facility today and he can go there in the morning. "Dr. Dixon said. "No Dr. Dixon, it's okay. I guess he can come home with us. My two children would think I'm the worst person in the world to let their dad go to a place like that, knowing he may need us and our support." I said. "Okay. I'll set everything up and he'll be ready to come home tomorrow morning." Dr. Dixon said. "Thank you," I replied, walking off.

CHAPTER

32

Another Day

Adrienne and Sharese came by the hospital to be with us. I really appreciate their support and them being here with us. Adrienne said she'll take the kids home to grab some things for school tomorrow and they can spend the night at her house. I told Adrienne I really appreciate that and them both being here for us.

Adrienne and Sharese left about twenty minutes ago. I don't talk to Jason's parents anymore but I decided to call his mom to at least tell her what was going on. I know Mrs. Davis has never really cared for me, probably because I'm that sister that doesn't hold my tongue and will tell her ass off when she says something slick to me. Jason's dad Mr. Davis is okay but has a wandering eye for the ladies as well, so I see where Jason gets it from.

I dialed Mrs. Davis phone number and waited for her to answer the phone. "Hello Jannice. How are you?" Mrs. Davis asked. "I'm doing okay." I said. "How's my grandchildren doing?" Mrs. Davis asked. "They're just fine but a little shaken up." I said. "Shaken up?" Mrs. Davis asked. "Yes, that's the reason why I'm calling you. Jason was shot a few hours ago in the back. Someone tried to rob him and he's in the hospital now. The bullet went straight through and just missed his spine." I said. "Oh my God child. Why didn't you call me earlier?" Mrs. Davis asked. "I'm calling you now." I said.

Mrs. Davis sucked her teeth. "Where are the children?" Mrs. Davis asked. "They're spending the night with my best friend Adrienne." I said. "Don't you think you should all be together as a family?" Mrs. Davis asked. "Mrs. Davis, the doctor says that Jason should be coming home tomorrow morning. So I'll ask him if he wants to stay there with you or come to my house." I said, ignoring her question. "Don't you mean his house?" Mrs. Davis said, as I imagined her rolling her neck around. "Have a great day Mrs. Davis." I said, hanging up the phone.

I'm so proud of myself for not letting this woman get the best of me. Before I give her that, I'll hang up in her face first. I went to Jason's room to sit with him for a bit before I leave for the night. Jason was watching TV when I walked in. "Hey there." I said, grabbing his hand. "Hey Jannice. How are you?" Jason asked. "I'm fine but I should be asking you that." I said. "Well I'm okay. I'm just in a little pain that's all." Jason said. "Well that's good." I said.

Jason turned the TV volume down. "Where are the kids?" Jason asked. "Adrienne came by and wanted to take them to her house to spend the night. I agreed to it. They've been through a lot today." I said. "Yes, I agree." Jason said. "I called your mother." I said. "Oh Lord, how did she react?" Jason asked. "You know your mother. She probably thinks I'm the one that shot you or hired someone to do it." I said. "Yeah. I'm sure she probably does. Did she say whether they were coming by to see me?" Jason asked. "No She didn't. But knowing your mother, I'm sure she will." I said. "You're right." Jason replied.

The nurse came in to check Jason's vitals. The nurse looked familiar when she looked up at me. "It's good to see you first lady. Oh how we missed you." The young nurse said. "Oh my, I thought you looked familiar." I said. "Jannice this is Mrs. Shirley Mae and Mr. Hazel's granddaughter Tammy." Jason said. "Oh my God. Look at you." I said, as I hugged Tammy tightly. "How is your grandparents doing?" I asked. "They're doing good." Tammy said. "Isn't Martha your mother?" I asked. "Yes she is." Tammy said. "I hope she is doing well." I said. "She is." Tammy said.

"Please tell Mrs. Shirley Mae and Mr. Hazel I said hello and that I sure miss them." I said. "I sure will. You take care first lady and I'll be praying for your family." Tammy said. "Thank you sweetheart. Tammy, I'm so proud of the young lady you turned out to be. You're an RN and doing good. Just remember to keep God first in everything you do and he will direct your path." I said. "I sure will first lady. You all take care." Tammy said, as she left the room.

It was so good to see Tammy and see how well she turned out. "I love to see our young people do so well at our church." I said. "Yes, It's truly a blessing." Jason said. "Look, the doctor said you can come home in the morning. Do you want to go back to your apartment or your parents? If you want, you can come back to the house and stay in the guest room. I'm sure the kids will be glad to have you there so they can help get you certain things that you need." I said. "What about you? Will you be glad to have me there?" Jason asked.

I decided to be a little more mindful of what I say to Jason, before I curse him out. "I'm just doing this to help you out some and the kids will be glad to have you there as well." I said. "Well, I don't want to be a burden for you." Jason said. "Please Jason. What do you want to do?" I asked, not entertaining his foolishness. "Okay, I think I want to stay with you and the kids until I get better." Jason said. "Okay but remember this is just temporary. Please don't get comfortable. Call me tomorrow when they dismissed you and I'll come get you and bring you to the house." I said. "Do you think you can pick up my car from CiCi's? It's just sitting in their parking lot. "Jason said. "Okay, I'll get someone to take me to get it tomorrow. Look, you have a goodnight." I said.

Jason sat up in bed, as if he didn't like what I said. "You're leaving Jannice? You're not going to stay the night with me?" Jason asked. I just looked at Jason like he just lost his damn mind. "Jason, you must have forgot that we're no longer married. You should call one of your damn tricks over to take care of you and nurse you back to health. It amazes me how people can go out there with the trash on the street but when something happens, they expect the wife or that loyal person to take care of them. Why can't you call on that person you were cheating with and spending your time with? Where the hell are they now that you need them?" I asked.

I didn't give Jason a chance to respond as I grabbed my purse and walked out his room. I don't know if this will be a good idea to let Jason move back in temporarily. Maybe he should go stay with his parents until he's back on his feet, because I'm not up for fooling up with his ass any longer. I'm only doing it for the kids.

I got inside my car and just started thanking God for his protection and how he kept Jason and my children safe. If the devil had his way and Jason hadn't risked his own life to save our children, then they might not have been here. Thank you God for keeping Jason and our children another day.

CHAPTER

33

Is This What You Want?

Jason's been back in the house for a week now. The doctor set up for Jason to have his physical therapy at the house instead of going to the rehabilitation center. He seems like he's doing better and able to walk a little longer each day. He's even able to stand up longer than before as well. I think after another week he should be able to go back to his own place sooner I hope.

Marcus has been very understanding about me letting Jason move back home to help him get back on his feet. We haven't been seeing much of each other, other than two lunch dates this week but he asked to take me out on a real date tonight and I agreed. It would be good to get out the house for a change and get all dolled up.

Ricardo tried to come by my office the other day and I told the receptionist to tell him that we don't have anything to talk about and the next time he comes to the school, I'll have him escorted off the premises.

My receptionist Ms. Laura told me that Ricardo didn't take the news well when she relayed the message to him. I told her that Ricardo messed up, and I'm not up for giving anyone else a pass to hurt me again. Jason was enough and now I have his ass back in my damn house again, like nothing never happened to get us to this place.

I decided to make dinner tonight. Jason loves my spaghetti and meatballs. I'll make that for dinner and bring him some to his room. I had the kitchen smelling all good. The kids washed up for dinner and sat at the table. Jason walked to the kitchen with his cane and sat down at the table with us. He's been doing so good and I'm actually proud of his progress of how well he's doing. I put their dinner on the table and then headed upstairs to get ready.

I jumped in the shower and then got dressed. I know Jason is probably hating the fact that I'm moving on without him but I am. I'm going to let him stay one more week here and then I think he'll be ready to go back to his apartment.

I pinned up my hair and made sure everything was intact before I headed downstairs. I hugged and kissed the kids before, I headed out the door. "You're not going to say anything to me?" Jason asked. "Yes, goodnight and I'll see you later on." I said, walking out the house. I'm sure I get on Jason's last nerves but he can always go back home when he's ready to. I'm not stopping him at all.

Marcus told me to meet him at Red Lobster. I texted him that I was just pulling up. Marcus and I haven't discussed how we're going to dress for dinner. I just hope I'm not overdressed or anything.

I got out the car and was heading to the door. I saw Marcus, standing in some khaki pants, a nice casual brown shirt, and a dark blue blazer. He looks very nice. Marcus isn't exactly a ten or anything but from a scale from one to ten, I would give him a seven. He's okay on the eyes, he's about six feet tall, dark-skinned and has a low wavy haircut. Marcus looks like Mr. Brown from the Tyler Perry plays.

Marcus must have started working out recently because he's a lot more tone than he used to be. "Hey there." I said, walking up to him. "Hello Jannice. How are you doing?" Marcus asked, as he kissed me on the lips and then hugged me tightly. His kiss caught me off guard but I didn't mind it at all. "It's good to see you." I said. "Likewise Jannice. I have something to tell you that you won't believe me when I tell you." Marcus said, smiling. "Huh? And what's that?" I asked. "You'll find out soon enough Jannice." Marcus said, with a little sly grin on his face.

I followed Marcus to our table and looked at our menu. I know I wasn't up for a huge meal so I just decided on a crab salad, which comes with the bread sticks. The waitress came and took our order.

Marcus kept his eyes on me the entire time, with a smile on his face. "So what is it you had to tell me?" I asked, curious to know. "Okay, do you remember that wedding we all went to twelve years ago? It was Deidra and Neil's wedding." Marcus said. "Yes I do. Deidra is my cousin and Neil is you and Jason's friend right?" I asked. "Yes, that's true. Jannice, the moment you walked down the aisle as your cousin maid of honor, I couldn't keep my eyes off you. I turned to Jason, who was sitting beside me and I told him that young lady is going to be my wife. Jason just laughed at me. He actually had his eye on another girl Tamia but he found out that she had a boyfriend. Now, I ate something at the reception that didn't agree with my stomach and I must have stayed in the bathroom for about thirty to forty minutes.

When I came out the restroom you and Jason were talking at the table. You two looked really comfortable talking and I was fucking pissed. I introduced myself to you and then left so you two could talk. Jason called me the next day bragging and saying that I was moving too slow for him so he had to step up his game. I cursed him out and we didn't talk for two weeks. Jannice, this was the type of shit Jason did all the time in our entire childhood. Whatever I wanted, he tried his best to beat me to it, just to prove that he could.

Jannice the day you two got married, you don't know how I cried and cried, wishing that I was the one marrying you instead of Jason, knowing he didn't deserve you. That's why I refused to be his best man when he first asked me to. I couldn't even be in one of my so called friend's wedding because he was marrying the woman I was in love with. I hated him that day even more then the day he beat me to meeting you first." Marcus said.

I immediately felt the tears forming in my eyes as I quickly grabbed a napkin to catch my tears. I was absolutely devastated. I felt that someone just knocked the wind out of me and I was lying flat on the floor. "Why are you crying?" Marcus asked. "Because I could've been with someone that would've love and cherish me instead of someone who cheated and neglected me." I said. "That was the second worst thing I regretted when I found out he was cheating on you." Marcus said. "Marcus, why didn't you tell me?" I asked. "I felt like that really wasn't my place but I did tell you, just not in my own voice." Marcus said.

Now Marcus had me confuse as hell, and I had no idea what he meant. "What do you mean not in your own voice?" I asked. "Do you remember the woman that called you the first time and told you, if you want your husband he was at Super 8?" Marcus asked. "Yes I do," I said. "That was my sister. I asked her to do it and even though she didn't want to, she did it." Marcus said. "Wow, was all I could say. I think it's time for you to get this bastard out your house as soon as possible." Marcus said. "I agree. I'm going to let him stay this last week and Sunday, he's going back to his place." I said. "Good." Marcus replied.

Marcus and I ate dinner and enjoyed each other's conversation. Marcus is really a great guy and I swear if I knew then what I know now, my life would probably be different right now. I guess I'll never know about the past but I'm sure hoping we can spend our future together.

CHAPTER

34

Get The Hell Out

The children and I were lying on the couch in the den watching "The Lion King." The children love this movie and I must admit this is one of my favorite animated movies as well. I've watched this movie probably about fifty times and I never get tired of it. Jason's been in his room the entire time. He's been a little quiet today since I got home from work. I wanted so badly to ask about him calling himself beating Marcus to me at Deidra and Neil's wedding, but I didn't. There was no need because it's not like the bastard would ever admit to what he's done anyway.

Jason made dinner tonight, which was actually pretty good. I told Jason I would do the dishes tonight, since he cooked dinner. I normally just put them in the dishwasher but since I wasn't doing anything. I was going to wash them the old fashion way. Jason is now walking without even using his cane. He told me he was able to walk all day without using it. He said he's ready to go back to work because working from home is way too boring for him. I told him if he's ready to go back, he should.

I got up off the couch to wash the dishes, when the doorbell ring. Who the hell is that at this hour. I glanced up at the clock in the kitchen and it was only eight-thirty. I went to the door and saw this strange man standing there.

I opened the door partially to ask the man what he wanted. "Hello. May I help you?" I asked. "Hello ma'am, I'm here to see Jason." The man said. "Okay, hold on for a second, I'll get him for you." I said, closing my front door back shut.

I knocked on Jason's door. "Hey Jannice. What's up?" Jason asked. "Jason, there's someone at the door for you. Please don't have people coming to my house like that. Your little friend looks like a thug." I said.

Jason walked towards the door and I went in the kitchen. "Hey man, what are you doing here?" Jason asked, like he was scared or something. I could tell this man was someone that Jason had no idea was coming over here. "Come on in. We can talk on the back porch." Jason said, inviting the man inside. Jason and the man headed outside and as soon as he walked through the back door and walked on the porch, I ran behind them and cracked the back door open so I could listen to their conversation, because something isn't right and I can feel it.

The man was standing in front of Jason. "Dude, what the hell do you get off coming to my damn house like this?" Jason asked. "Man, you didn't leave me any choice since you haven't been answering my calls or text messages." The man said. "Look Lee, don't you ever come to my damn house again!" Jason yelled! "Look fool. You owe me the other seven thousand dollars. I don't think you want me to go inside and tell your little family that you were the one who set that entire robbery shit up and that it was your idea for me to shoot you in the back? Your wife might not be to thrill to know you did all this, just for her to let you back in the house to try and get your family back together. How would your children feel, knowing what their father did to them? Traumatizing them like that. I swear to God, I'll go in there right now and tell them everything." The man said.

I wanted to scream. Who the hell does Jason think his ass is playing. I tried to stay calm, because I wanted to hear the rest of this conversation. "Lee, prove it! No one would believe a fucking crackhead addict!" Jason yelled.

The man laughed out loudly. "Yes Jason, I'm a crackhead but I promise you, I'm a smart ass crackhead. I figure you would say who would believe me, so that's why I recorded our conversation when you had me set it up for that day when you called me to meet you at CiCi's. I even had someone video us while the supposed to be robbery was taking place. They recorded it with their phone then they sent it to me. And that's why I recorded this conversation that we're having now." The man said, as he reached in his jacket pocket and pulled out his cell phone. "Damn, he had Jason ass right where he wanted him and he had no other choice but to give this Lee man exactly what he wanted. "Okay, I'll write you a check." Jason said. "The hell you won't write me no damn check, for you to put a damn stop on it and have me looking like I stole the damn check from you at the bank. Come on Jason you have to do better than that. I'm no damn fool." The man said.

Jason had no idea that he wasn't dealing with an amateur here. This Lee man knows exactly what he's doing. He had all his ducks in a row and he was playing the game quite well. Shit, hell this Lee man could teach my ass a thing or two.

I walked upstairs to my room and went in my closet. I opened the lockbox that I had in the top of my closet and got my 9mm gun and took out some emergency money that I keep just in case of a rainy day. I put the gun between my pants and pulled my shirt down over it so the kids wouldn't see it when I walk back downstairs. I'm about to set some shit off.

I walked through the den and the kids were watching TV. "Jay and Myra, it's time to go to bed." I said. "Mom, can we stay up a little longer?" Jay asked. "I said go to bed and if I come back in here and you're still sitting on that couch, it won't be good for neither one of you. Do not come down those stairs for nothing unless I call you." I said, with a stern tone.

Jay and Myra turned the TV off and ran upstairs like I asked them to. I put my cell phone in my back pocket and pulled the gun out my pants, while I walked on the back porch, closing the back door behind me. "Jannice, what are you doing out here?" Jason asked. I pointed the gun at them both. "Wait a minute! Wait a minute! Jason what is your crazy ass wife doing?" The man yelled. "I'm about to blow both your sorry asses away." I said.

Jason tried walking towards me and I aim the gun by him and fired a shot. I missed him but I wanted him to know I meant business. The man screamed. "Ah Shit! I just pissed my damn pants," the man said. "So what you gonna do, shoot us both?" Jason asked. "I don't plan to unless I don't get what I want." I said. "So what do you want?" Jason asked. I was listening to your entire conversation so I know what you both did. Now sir, what you're going to do is email both of those recordings and the video to my email that you and my husband planned with you shooting my husband in the back in front of my children or the next bullet is going straight through you. Please try me if you think I'm bullshitting." I said.

The man looked at me like he had seen a ghost. "Damn Jason, your wife is straight up fucking crazy!" the man said. "Yep, I sure am. Now are you going to do like I ask?" I said. "What is your email shorty?" the man asked. I gave the man my email and he started doing something in his phone. "It's sent." The man said. I took my phone out my pocket and checked my email. The video and recording was there.

I took out two thousand dollars out my pocket and handed it to the man. "That's two thousand dollars I just handed you. Now that's your pay for what you just gave me. Now if I ever catch you anyway near me, my children, or my house ever again, that bullet you just heard that I missed my husband with, I promise you, I won't miss you. Jason, will be giving you the rest of your seven thousand dollars tomorrow. Do you understand?" I asked. "Yes, I do," the man said. "Good, now get the fuck away from my house and don't you ever come back again." I yelled. "Gladly! You a crazy ass bitch!" The man said, almost tripping over himself as he ran off my back porch.

I kept the gun on Jason. "I swear there's no hope for your ass! Tomorrow, you're going to pay that bastard the rest of that seven thousand you owe him and Jason, if I find out you didn't, I'm taking this video and the recording straight to the damn police. I doubt if you want your church to know what kind of pastor they have and it would be hard to preach behind bars, unless you're going to start a prison ministry in there. You have twenty minutes to get your shit and get the hell out of my house. I'm sorry I even met your stupid ass." I said, walking upstairs.

CHAPTER

35

Six Months Later

It's been six months now since Jason has been out of my house for good. After that guy Lee came over and exposed Jason and sent me the information he had on him, he hasn't tried to maneuver his way back into my life, with anymore underhanded tricks.

It's been a lot of things that happened within these last six months. Nicolas asked Adrienne to marry him and we're both over the moon happy for them. Adrienne has been unhappy for years since her bitter divorce and her alcohol addiction, but look at her now. Home girl is striving on her new job as school superintendent, and looking forward to her wedding. That smile that Nicolas has put on her face, seemed like it was engraved there for good and it's been nothing but a blessing.

Nicolas can't stop thanking me for inviting him to my divorce celebration, because he doesn't think that he and Adrienne paths would've crossed again. I told Nicolas if it was in God's plan, then he would've worked it all out for both of them to be at the right place and at the right time. I do enjoy taking a little credit in seeing the smile and the love they express to each other. Their wedding is set for the day after Valentine's Day, on February 15.

Sharese and Scott are my idea couple. They got married three months ago in the Bahamas. Only Sharese's closes relatives and friends were there. Adrienne and I were right there by her side the entire time. Sharese has been through a lot when she was diagnosed with breast cancer five years ago and the death of her father. When she told us about Scott and that she met the man of her dreams and that he completes her. It warmed my heart to see that glow on her face. There's nothing like true love that will bring out the best in anybody and it certainly has with them.

Sharese just announced to us last week that she and Scott were expecting their first child. Adrienne and I looked at each other and we had the same exact reaction, we both burst out in tears. Sharese ran to us and hugged us both tightly. Adrienne and I always knew that Sharese would be a great mother but Sharese never thought that a child would be in the works for her, especially after the doctors told her after her battle with cancer it would be nearly impossible for her to conceive. Sharese never gave up hope and neither did Adrienne and I. We knew that with God on her side he could turn the doctors "no" into his "yes." We have a new addition that's coming into our lives and we're so happy about it.

I was watching the news the other day and it showed a huge drug bust of a truck driver, that was smuggling drugs in the United States through their product. I almost brought up my food when they said the person's name, as Ricardo James. The news said someone tipped off the police that a large supply was coming through. Ricardo's four men were sentenced to thirty-five years and Ricardo was sentenced to fifty years, I guess since he was the one that was in charge of the drug operation. I knew Ricardo was dirty but I allowed my eyes to see what my heart was telling me no to. I tried giving Ricardo the benefit of the doubt that he was no longer selling drugs but if he wasn't honest about being a single man, then why in the hell did I expect him to have been honest about not selling drugs anymore. I guess I was just hoping for something different with him, other than the lies and cheating that I was accustomed with from Jason.

I promised myself that I would never carry anything old into something new that I'm starting with someone. That's not fair to that person you can't go through life blaming the person that's in your life now for something your ex or an old boyfriend did years ago. In order for a person to walk into a new door of opportunity, they have to close the door of the old one. You can't keep looking back once you close the door. Once that door is closed, let it go.

I've learned to let everything go for how Ricardo and Jason treated me, and I'm allowing Marcus to love me the way I deserve to be loved. Marcus and I sat the kids down to explain to them how we feel about each other. Marcus was glad to see the kids because after he and Jason stopped talking, he hasn't seen the kids since then. Myra was only a few months old then so she doesn't remember him the way Jay does.

Jay said he was glad to have Marcus back in his life but he had to remember to stop calling him "Uncle Marcus" and now just Marcus. I asked Marcus last night did he see marriage in our future and he said, he wanted nothing more than anything to marry me and be my husband.

Jason found out that Marcus and I were together but of course he was upset about it but I told him he better enjoy his life and all his many women because he messed up what he had and now another man, a good man has what he neglected.

I cuddled up beside Marcus and the kids on the couch and we all watched "spider man." I couldn't help but to smile when I looked back from where I started when I caught Jason over at that woman's house. I wanted to give up on love but if I did, I would've never find out the truth about Marcus and how he really felt about me. It's funny how life can throw you a curve ball and change your entire life around, when you thought it was heading down one way and it ends up down a totally different path. Jason might have bruised me but he didn't break me. I'm glad that I allowed myself to heal, otherwise I may have never found what God has in stored for me. I know my worth and I'll never allow anyone to treat me other than the queen that I am. What some may see as trash, someone else will value as a treasure and that's how Marcus sees and treats me.

The End, By John D. McCray

Printed in the USA
CPSIA information can be obtained
at www.ICGtesting.com
LVHW020933150524
780224LV00016B/813

9 781962 611619